Summer
AND THE GROOMSMAN

CATHRYN HEIN

A South Australian country girl by birth, Cathryn loves nothing more than a rugged rural hero who's as good with his heart as he is with his hands, which is probably why she writes them! Her romances are warm and emotional, and feature themes that don't flinch from the tougher side of life but are often happily tempered by the antics of naughty animals. Her aim is to make you smile, sigh, and perhaps sniffle a little, but most of all feel wonderful.

Cathryn was born horse mad, which is little wonder with three generations of jockeys in the family. After scoring her first horse at age 10, upon whom she bestowed the eternally romantic name of Mysty, Cathryn spent the rest of her teenage years in equine bliss riding pony club and hunt club, and competing in eventing, dressage and showjumping until university beckoned.

Armed with a shiny Bachelor of Applied Science (Agriculture) from Roseworthy College she moved to Melbourne and later Newcastle, working in the agricultural and turf seeds industry. Her partner's posting to France took Cathryn overseas for three years in Provence where she finally gave in to her life-long desire to write.

All of Cathryn's novels have been finalists in the Australian Romance Readers Awards and the 2014 awards also saw her in contention for Favourite Australian Romance Author.

Cathryn currently lives in New South Wales at the base of the Blue Mountains with her partner of many years, Jim. When she's not writing, she plays golf (ineptly), cooks (well), and in football season barracks (rowdily) for her beloved Sydney Swans AFL team.

cathrynhein.com

Summer and the Groomsman

Also by Cathryn Hein

The Falls
Rocking Horse Hill
Heartland
Heart of the Valley
Promises
The French Prize

For Jim

ONE

Harry Argyle never saw the horse. Not fully. He saw something with a huge black arse and, knowing that hitting things with big arses never turned out pretty, he swerved. A sideways skid and spray of gravel later and his ute was nose down in the overgrown gutter that ran alongside Redbank Road – the one the district council never mowed or repaired no matter how many times he complained – and repeating a word that'd earn him a solid clip over the ear from his mum, should she hear it.

He swore again to dispel the last traces of his shock and jammed the ute into reverse, easing it out of the gutter and back onto the unsealed road. Fat arse had turned around and now stood blinking at the headlights and puffing steam into the cold night, and regarding Harry as if he was the anomaly in this scene.

"A horse. Jesus." He scratched his head and stared at it.

The dumb thing took a step forward, its fine ears at attention. He could see now that its coat wasn't black but a rich dark brown. A white star shone in the middle of its forehead.

"To line up where the bullet goes," muttered Harry, although he didn't mean it. He liked horses. They reminded him a bit of himself: not the smartest animals in the world, but big, brown-eyed, friendly, and kind of sweet.

He changed into neutral and left the car to idle. Outside the warm interior the night had chilled considerably. Sign of another fine one tomorrow. It was almost November and so far spring in this lower south-eastern corner of South Australia had been perfect. Periodic soaking rains followed by sunshiny days that stimulated the pasture and left his family's stud Simmentals grazing in lush, knee-high grass.

The horse whickered a soft equine hello and took a step forward. Harry scanned the road, checking for other cars. The moon was a thin crescent, the southern constellations bright, the night inky. Only his headlights lit the narrow country road. Redbank Road tended to be the reserve of local property owners and the occasional hoon looking for a patch of gravel on which to practice being a dickhead, but even they'd been put off by the potholes that pockmarked the surface, thanks to a wet winter. Harry used it on his trips into town from the farm because he liked the quiet, plus it took him past Maya Higgins's house, allowing him to wistfully wonder what she was dreaming about in her bed. Wishing it was him.

The horse took another couple of steps toward him. Harry walked closer and held out his hand for the horse to sniff, then stroked its nose, smiling in spite of himself. From its docility he figured it was someone's riding horse. He scanned its body as best as he could in the headlights. Frowning, he crouched to inspect the animal's forelegs closer. The horse sniffed and nuzzled Harry's hair as he reached out to trace the cut marks. They didn't look too bad, superficial scratches from barbed wire probably. He glanced across the road toward old Gav's farm. Gav was a drunken no-hoper who did nothing to upkeep the property he'd inherited by default from his uncle thirty years before. Every time Harry looked at the place he seethed at the waste.

He rose and with another light pat of the horse headed back to the ute for a torch, wishing Lucy was in the back so he could let her off to go sniffing. But his kelpie was at home with the other dogs, sleeping off a day's activity.

He directed the torchlight across the road and studied the fence line, searching for a breach. Even in the darkness the shocking state of Gav's farm was obvious. So sagged were some of the wires that the animal could have crossed at any number of places. He eyed the horse again and shone the torch over its flanks. Could be a jumper given its build, not that the fence would pose much of a challenge, especially for a horse with a hankering for green feed. Something Gav's place lacked badly.

Harry swept the light across the other side of the road just to make sure. He needn't have bothered. That land belonged to the Davidsons and they were pretty smart operators. Their twin girls were toddlers, not even at the pony-riding stage, and Harry doubted they'd offer horse agistment, whereas old Gav would chase every cent he could get. Plus Harry thought he'd seen the horse before when he'd passed. Just a glimpse of its hindquarters as it ambled over the hill, but definitely at Gav's.

With a sigh he turned off the torch and dumped it on the ute's bonnet before unbuckling his belt and threading it out of the loops of his jeans. He circled the leather around the horse's neck, making a clicking noise with his tongue as he tugged. After a yearning glance toward the opposite paddock, the horse dropped his head in resignation and followed like a dopey puppy.

Away from the headlights, Harry waited for his eyes to adjust to the night. On Gav's side of the road the grass was tall and rank; great tussocks of phalaris and Victoria ryegrass mixed with swathes of bracken that hadn't seen a slasher in years. The horse trailed him along the road edge, a great amiable bulk of warmth at Harry's shoulder. At the far end of the paddock a fencepost listed heavily outwards, its base almost rotted through, its collapse prevented only by three strands of loose barbed wire. The horse wouldn't have even needed to jump. A couple of steps would have done it, although one misstep and it could have knotted itself in a disastrous tangle.

Harry stood studying the fence, the horse calmly by his side as though in shared contemplation. This needed more tools than he had at hand, but he could manage enough of a running repair to keep the animal safe at least for the night. Releasing another disgruntled huff, he led the horse back to the gate and through, unwrapped his belt, and gave its silky coat another pat. He watched it for a moment as it shook its head and ambled away, sniffing the ground, then he latched the gate and headed back to the ute.

Harry had pliers and baling twine and not much else, but if he could tighten the wires enough, maybe string a bit of orange twine, it'd at least hold the post up. The horse hung close as he worked, its eyes catching the shine of the moon, strangely comforting. Satisfied he'd done all he could, Harry gave the horse a last nose rub, cast a filthy look toward the farmhouse, and strode back to his car.

***

"For fuck's sake!"

Harry slammed the brakes of his ute as once again the tyres skidded on the gravel. At least today the horse wasn't on the road. He stood at the edge, oblivious, happily tucking into a patch of purple flowering lucerne. Not that it needed the extra feed. Clearly someone was looking after it – a horse couldn't get that fit and sleek on Gav's pastures alone.

Good thing Harry had decent tools in the tray, not that he should have to repair Gav's bloody fence anyway. That was the landowner's responsibility, but relying on the old drunk was a waste of time. Something the horse's owner should surely know by now. Cattle and sheep could be problems enough, but horses, with their flighty, dumb natures, could cause all sorts of havoc. What if it'd been hoons driving along the road, or a young mum distracted by her children? Or Maya? Could've been a disaster.

The thought made Harry fume. It pissed him off mightily that people could be so irresponsible. Whoever owned this animal needed a good kick up the arse, and when Harry found out who it was he planned to let rip.

He spent half an hour going over the roadside fence, cursing for most of it, and wondering why he was wasting his time. But if he didn't do it he suspected it simply wouldn't get done, and it wasn't the horse's fault. He'd hate to see the animal hurt because he was too absorbed in his own grumpiness to do the right thing.

Satisfied, he headed to Gav's place, determined to take his mood out on someone.

The old man took his time answering. Noises echoed within. Muttered curses and things being knocked. The door opened a crack, emitting a disgusting whiff of sweat and alcohol tinged with a sour undercurrent of urine. Another blast of fury at the horse owner thundered through Harry. It was probably the agistment fees that were keeping Gav in booze.

"Yeah?"

"Who owns the horse, Gav?"

The old man rubbed his eyes, his raised arm releasing a waft of body odour. "Young girl. Why?"

"Because the bloody thing keeps getting out. Twice this week."

Gav looked at him as if to say "So?"

"You need to fix that fence. With the road the way it is someone could get killed."

"I'll get onto it," said Gav in a way that revealed he'd heard all this before and knew what answer to give, but his weary, couldn't-give-a-rat's-arse tone shone through.

"When?" Harry persisted.

"Next couple of days."

He began to push the door shut. Harry stuck his size thirteen foot against it. "Make sure you do."

"Yeah, yeah."

"I'll be back to check."

Gav's gaze, until now rheumy and uncaring, developed a touch of steel. Harry matched it with an expression equally as tough, and from a bloke who stood a shade short of two metres tall and weighed over a hundred kilos, tough had serious meaning. Gav looked away first.

Message delivered, Harry removed his boot. The door slammed shut immediately. He took a few steps away and inhaled, grateful for the fresh air.

What made a man get like that?

He shook his head. How the old soak treated himself was no business of his, but the moment he put others in danger, especially people Harry cared about, that was a different matter. Maya used this road. If anything happened to her he'd never forgive himself.

***

Summer Taylor checked the fence with delight. Her desperate entreaties to Gav must have finally triggered the man to action. Although makeshift, all the top strands of the fence were in place, while the rotting post that keep toppling over was fixed upright, thanks to a well-hammered star dropper and a base packed tight with soil. Not perfect by any means, but enough to keep Binky where he belonged.

With her horse tied securely to the gnarly old pine she used as a makeshift hitching rail, Summer opened the gate and drove into the paddock, smiling with affection at Binky as he stared longingly toward his escape route. The greedy guts could sniff lucerne from a mile off and the horse was forever trying to sneak through the gate to get to the volunteer plants that sprouted along the opposite verge of the road.

She parked her SUV on the safe side of Gav's hay shed. The posts holding it up listed westward so alarmingly that Summer was always surprised to find it still standing. It was dangerous, but the only shelter available to store Binky's hard feed. His precious bales of hay she kept under a heavy tarpaulin in front, with a double-stranded electric fence surrounding the lot. For a while she'd contemplated using large concrete pavers to keep the tarp in place, and moving the electric fence to the paddock's front boundary, but experience had taught her Binky was an expert at finding ways into feed, no matter how well covered. With premium lucerne going for well over ten dollars a bale, hay was too expensive to squander and money was tight. Feeding Binky was costing her a small fortune as it was and Summer couldn't afford any wastage.

Binky stamped and shuffled as she fetched a casserole dish off the car's rear seat. Backing out, Summer blew kisses his way. "Patience, baby." A bump of her hip shut the car door and with a duck through another loosely wired fence, she carried the casserole toward Gav's house.

A chook shot off into the backyard's long grass, squawking. Hidden beneath an unclipped box hedge, a calico cat lurked, attention tuned for birds. Summer hissed, scaring the cat off, and made a mental reminder to find a collar with a bell for it.

She knocked and called out, waiting a moment before pushing the door open a sliver. "Gav? It's Summer."

Creaks sounded from further in the house. She sniffed cautiously, wondering how bad it would be, but the air was free of the rank stench of vomit that had been there two days prior. Anguish rose in her chest. He'd probably run out of money to pay for booze, and now she was going to hand over her agistment fee.

Except what was she meant to do? She couldn't not

pay him. Nor was she responsible for Gav's alcoholism. With limited resources, all Summer could do was show some human kindness. Although that didn't make it easier to bear. Or remove the guilt.

"Gav, I'm coming in. I've brought you chicken and veg pie. I'll just put it in the oven to heat, okay?"

She pushed the door open wider and surveyed the kitchen. Dishes lined the sink. A couple of empty mugs were on the kitchen table, the local Levenham Leader newspaper nearby. Clean, by Gav's standards.

In the background she could hear the faint trickle of water. Summer headed for the oven and cranked it on before sliding the foil-covered casserole inside. By the time she'd finished with Binky, Gav's meal would be ready and she'd have a few minutes to chat and ensure he would receive at least some decent nutrition.

Everything set, she slipped back outside.

Binky stood stoically under the tree as she saddled him. The early evening was hushed, almost lonely sounding, and not for the first time Summer wished for home. For the landscape she'd grown up with, her friends, her mum and dad and two brothers. The safety of familiarity. But unless she wanted to continue the rest of her life unemployed and sponging off her parents, or stuck doing a job she hated, Levenham would have to do. It wasn't perfect but she'd scored a good position with a reputable business and, compared to the last disaster, that was a major plus.

Binky nudged her shoulder as she tapped the top of his off foreleg. She lifted it up and drew it gently toward her, stretching and smoothing the skin beneath the saddle's girth. After repeating the same exercise with his

14

nearside leg, she gave him a last pat, put her foot in the stirrup, and vaulted lightly into the saddle.

Sunset was already drifting in, dappling the paddocks in peach and saffron, and granting Gav's bracken-infested pastures a strange dusky prettiness. Summer would have preferred to take Binky for a long walk around the roads, get him away from the boredom of the farm, but her last client had arrived late and then a staff meeting had delayed her further.

She urged Binky into his silky trot. It was the beautiful dark bay coat that seemed to shimmer when he moved that had first attracted Summer to him, but it was the sheer elegance of his paces that sealed the deal – a beautiful floaty trot that made Binky look like he was walking on air. In extended trot he seemed to skate, as if the ground was made of ice and he was surging across it in sweeps.

Beyond Gav's boundary the surrounding lush paddocks were vivid in the failing light, their plants filling the air with a delicious herbaceous scent. Lucerne ready for cutting. Nitrogen-fixing white clover bright against the limier grasses. Shiny-leafed ryegrass. Duller fescue and cocksfoot. Gav's farm was like a crooked, ragged patch in an otherwise beautifully crafted quilt.

Summer exercised Binky near the rear fence, on the paddock's single strip of flat ground, practicing shoulder-ins, counter-canters and tight, ten metre circles, his snorts echoing in the country quiet. There wasn't a lot to like about Gav's farm but she appreciated its relative isolation and stillness. This felt peaceful and private, as if she and Binky were the only domesticated creatures left on earth. And it was a pleasant way to end a busy day.

The bracken was glowing a sickly hazel in the sun's last light when Summer ended her ride. She patted Binky's neck and walked him back to the hayshed, wondering if she could ask Gav to slash the paddock. She hoped her horse possessed enough nous not to eat the fern fronds, but with the other vegetation so poor there was a chance he might. A little was harmless, but too much could lead to thiamine deficiency and Binky staggering around like a drunk at a Bachelor and Spinster's Ball.

Summer dismounted and ran her hands over his coat, assessing his well-filled belly and rump. He seemed healthy enough but that would never stop her worrying. After unsaddling and brushing Binky down, she drew back the tarp protecting her stash of feed. The horse's nostrils flared and his dark brown eyes took on that pleading look she knew so well and adored, an almost childlike entreaty for "more, please". Summer levered off a couple of biscuits of lucerne hay and tossed them into a low rubber feed tub. Binky greedily tucked in, leaving her free to mix up his hard feed in another, smaller tub.

She placed the bucket alongside his hay and watched, amused, as Binky plunged his nose inside and closed his eyes in ecstasy. She scrubbed his mane as he munched, chattering affectionate nonsense, before returning to secure the feed and reactivate the electric fence.

Chores done and her horse happy, she headed back to the house.

Gav was at the kitchen table, a mug by his hand. His hair was still a little damp, his usually bristled jaw smooth. A woodsy scent hung in the air from the cologne he'd obviously applied.

Summer smiled. "You're looking perky."

"Going out."

The envelope in her pocket dug its pointed corner into her hip. Summer bet he was. As soon as his fingers closed around her agistment money he'd be off. With effort, she kept the dismay from her face and headed for the oven.

"You don't have to cook for me. I can take care of myself."

"I told you, it's leftovers. This girl can't live on tofu. I need meat."

Gav grunted. "Should be able to eat what you want in your own house."

"True, but it's not that easy." As Summer had discovered, much to her chagrin.

The last time Summer had brought home a thick rib steak for herself, on a night when her housemates Lissa and Lori were meant to be out, the girls had arrived home unexpectedly. A single glance at the table where the steak lay coming up to room temperature and Lissa had turned pale. Lori had clapped her hand over her mouth in horror before turning her angry gaze on Summer. If they hadn't been so desperate to share the rent on their big old house, Summer would have been out on her ear, regardless of the agreement they'd supposedly established before she'd moved in. Rental accommodation-seeking vegetarians were hard to come by in Levenham and circumstances meant they'd been forced to loosen their housemate criteria. Summer was allowed to cook meat whenever the girls were out, as long as she cleaned up and aired the place appropriately afterward. That they'd arrived home early was hardly her fault, but that hadn't stopped Lissa and Lori acting as though it was.

To keep the peace, Summer cooked herself pastas and stir-fries, and occasionally shared a meal with the others. Some were awful, others surprisingly tasty, but eventually her craving for meat would become too much. On those occasions, she'd cook enough for several helpings, stowing leftovers in plastic containers in the freezer, wrapped in foil to hide the contents from Lissa and Lori's delicate eyes. When Summer had started bringing Gav meals it was as much for her sake as his. She enjoyed a serve of protein without fear of offence, and Gav gained some much-needed nutrition.

She used tea towels to hold the hot casserole and carried it to the sink drainer. Enticing smells teased her nostrils and caused her stomach to rumble. Gav fetched plates for her and laid out cutlery and placemats on the table, adding salt, pepper and a bottle of tomato sauce to the centre.

Summer tried not to cringe at the sauce, but Gav had it with everything, as if that was the only flavour he could tolerate. Perhaps it was more to cover up the taste of vegetables. Or that his tastebuds had been desensitised by alcohol. Either way it didn't matter. He was eating, and that's what counted.

They sat down to their meal, neither feeling the need to talk. Summer had found the quiet disconcerting at first. Dinner at her parents' was always raucous, full of news and local gossip, mixed with the occasional good-hearted ribbing about Summer or her brothers' love lives. Or lack thereof in Summer's case. With Lissa and Lori, conversation was skewed mainly to politics, which her housemates adored and had strong opinions about, often in conflict with Summer's more conservative leanings. But she enjoyed the debate and was open-minded enough to appreciate a point well made.

With Gav it was the clink of cutlery, the occasional mutter about the weather or the local council, and the creak of the old house.

"You go," he said when they'd finished. "I'll wash up."

"No, I'll help. I want to take the dish home with me anyway."

She didn't need it. All she wanted was to delay his trip into the bottle shop for a little longer. She hadn't handed over her month's agistment money yet, though she'd caught Gav glancing at her pocket in expectation.

He washed fast, scrubbing with nervous energy, his desire oozing out of him the way alcohol would from his pores in the morning. Summer knew that smell too well – the stench of hopelessness and self-hatred. It had cost her grandfather his life.

Finally, when she could delay no longer, she pulled the envelope from her pocket and laid it on the table. She cast Gav a pleading look, but he was already slipping on a jacket and fetching the keys to his ute.

He caught her gaze and looked away, toward an old polished buffet and hutch and the gold-framed wedding portrait it held. His mouth worked for a moment, his eyes glazing, then he stared at the floor before looking up, not quite making eye contact.

"I'll see you tomorrow then."

"Sure," replied Summer. On impulse she stretched up and kissed Gav on the cheek, taking him by surprise.

"What was that for?"

"For fixing the front fence."

Bottom lip sucked in, he glanced aside again, crunching his keys in his fist. "Wouldn't want Binky getting hurt."

"No."

She patted his arm and opened the back door. Dark rambled, thick and ominous, causing a small shudder to course through her. Summer checked back over her shoulder, her voice soft. "Be careful, Gav."

Shame kept his head lowered.

Summer had barely reached the paddock gate when Gav reversed his ute out onto the road. She swung the gate open and turned her back as dismay yanked her insides. Thanks to her, Gav was about to destroy more of his body, not to mention his state of mind. She trudged back to the car, reminding herself that this wasn't her fault. That Gav wasn't her responsibility. He wasn't grandpa.

She slumped heavily in the driver's seat and put the SUV into gear, only for her dismay to worsen the moment she looked up.

"Binky!"

Taking advantage of her distraction, Binky was sauntering happily through the gate, his one-track mind intent on the lucerne growing so lushly on the other side of the road. Usually he could be relied on to stay by his feed buckets, but tonight his hunger for decent green feed proved too overwhelming.

Putting the car back into neutral, Summer snatched a lead rope off the back seat, alighted and strode after him, calling out. Usually he was easy to catch, but Binky appeared to be in one of his moods, and intent on playing funny buggers. Ignoring her, he tossed his head and broke into a trot.

Just as another car appeared through the dust left in Gav's wake.

"Binky!"

The driver braked hard. Gravel spewed from behind the vehicle's locked up wheels but the skid was flinging the car closer and closer to Binky.

Panicked, Summer ran after her horse, waving her arms in an attempt to scare him into a bolt. Anything to chase him out of danger. A horn blasted the night. The four-wheel drive veered, turned sideways on the road and spun, its massive bullbar just missing Summer's leg. Terror-stricken, she slipped on the loose stones and fell heavily onto her hands and knees.

The engine cut. A dust cloud hung. Then someone was running.

"Jesus Christ, are you all right?"

Summer looked up to find a giant standing over her. "Yes." She took a shuddery breath and assessed herself. Her heart was racketing painfully around her chest and her hands and knees throbbed. "Yes, I'm fine. Thanks."

The giant bent down and touched her elbow. "Here, let me help you up."

She squinted. With the car headlights behind him she couldn't see his face, only that he had short hair and slightly protruding ears. His voice was nice though, deep and masculine.

"It's okay. I can manage." Breathing hard, she stood and checked her grazed hands, then tested a couple of steps. Her skin and bruised knees hurt like blazes but her injuries were minor. She winced a reassuring smile. "I'm not hurt." And right now she was more worried about

Binky.

Summer limped toward him. The animal seemed oblivious to the drama it had caused. He raised his head at her approach, stems of lucerne disappearing inside his rapidly chewing mouth.

"This is your horse?" asked the giant.

"Yes." She patted Binky's neck while checking him over. Not a scratch. Typical. "I'm really sorry about this."

"Sorry? Sorry? What the fuck?"

Summer's eyes widened. Alarmed by the aggression in his tone and aware she was alone on a dark country road with a man twice her size, she braced herself and faced him fully. The dust was beginning to settle, eerie in the twilight. The light behind showed off the man's enormous silhouette; hands on his head, elbows wide, legs apart. No longer solicitous. Menacing.

Summer dug her fingers into a hunk of Binky's mane, watching warily.

He began to pace back and forth in front of the headlights, like a creepy character out of one of those lonely road urban legends. "You could have killed someone!"

"I'm sorry."

Suddenly he whirled around and strode toward her, finger jabbing. "This is the third fucking time! Sorry isn't good enough."

Her grip on Binky's mane tensed. Summer tried not to cringe at his proximity, at the fierceness of his body language and tone, even though her heart was jack-hammering and her own vulnerability was rapidly closing around her like a fist. She could see his features now. He was around her age perhaps, but with an old-fashioned look about him, thanks to his traditional haircut and prominent ears. But it was his fury that was terrifying.

"It was an accident."

He stared at her like she was an idiot. "The first time might have been an accident. The second was carelessness, but this," – he flung a hand toward Binky – "this is beyond irresponsibility. And what the fuck were you doing running after the stupid animal like that? I was this close" – he pinched his thumb and forefinger together – "to killing you!"

"I didn't think."

"That much is frigging obvious." He scanned her up and down, mouth curling slightly at the sight of her tight breeches, half-chaps and boots, before returning his contemptuous glare to hers. "Looks to me like you don't think too much about anything."

Tears began to prickle Summer's eyes but she was stuffed if she was going to show her distress in front of this pig of a man. Who did he think he was? It was an accident!

The apish bully directed a pointed finger at the paddock. "Look at that fence. You haven't even touched it."

"Gav said he'd get onto it. He's already made a few repairs."

The man let out a savage bark of laughter that carried no amusement at all. "Gav? That old drunk? He can't even thread his own belt." He took a step closer to Summer, his Olympic swimmer-sized shoulders cutting off the headlights' glow, leaving only emerging moonlight. Glittering eyes bored into hers. "Get that fence fixed before you kill someone."

Biting the inside of her lip, Summer held his gaze, her back straight. She forced her voice strong. "I'm sorry. It won't happen again."

"It had better not."

And with a final mean glare at her and Binky, he stomped back to his ute.

TWO

Harry stood in the foyer of Lush Spa and Beauty with his hands in his pockets and his weight shifting backward and forward from his heels to the balls of his feet, as if undecided whether to hang in or bolt. Standing with him was Josh Sinclair, the groom of the upcoming wedding party Harry was part of, and Digby Wallace-Jones, best man and soon-to-be Josh's brother-in-law. All three men were eyeing the shelves of feminine potions with trepidation, their noses slightly crinkled at the alien scent in the air. If the spa's aroma was anything to go by, this ordeal was going to leave them stinking like a florist's.

"I can't believe you agreed to this," Harry said to Josh.

His friend shrugged. "Didn't get much choice. Anyway, where's your sense of adventure?"

"Not here."

"Mum reckons we'll end up wanting to do it all the time," said Digby.

"Like hell." Harry shot a look at a poster promoting some sort of organic, pain-free waxing product and shuddered. "Why couldn't we have gone to the pub like a normal buck's party?"

"We're bonding," said Josh. "Finding our inner woman."

"Mate, it'd take a whole lot more than a facial to get

your inner woman up to speed."

"Speak for yourself, boofhead."

Harry caressed the left side of his flat chest and pouted. "I'm in touch with her."

Josh shot a look at Digby and let out a long sigh. "Pretty sad when a bloke has to fondle his own boobs for kicks, hey Dig?"

"It is."

Harry's hand dropped. "Bugger off, Sinclair."

Josh and Digby laughed. Well, that was at least something. Everyone knew Digby wasn't prone to much laughter these days. Couldn't blame him after the tragedy he'd suffered. Watching your fiancée lose her life in a quarry collapse while you were helpless to save her would screw with anyone's mind. If it weren't for Josh, who'd dragged an unconscious Digby to safety before attempting to rescue Felicity, Digby would likely be dead too.

Harry wandered over to the main window and stared out at the street. No sign of the girls, who were off getting their final dress fittings. A woman hurried past, glancing up in surprise as she spotted him through the glass. Harry took a quick step back. Smirking, she scuttled on, leaving Harry feeling even more of a twit.

After several nervous minutes, he finally spotted Josh's fiancée Emily Wallace-Jones striding along the street, and experienced a tug of envy. He'd known Em in school. Back then she'd been a pretty, if aloof, teenager but the woman she'd grown into was pure elegance and class. Harry's mum had hinted more than once about her eligibility, but Harry had never found that brand of cool containment attractive. Josh always had, and after a bit of drama the pair had found the kind of happiness Harry sought for himself. Except in his case the girl he'd been half in love with for the last two years wasn't interested. To make his envy even more poignant, last night his brother Eddie had mentioned Maya was seeing that no-hoper from the surf shop at Port Andrews, Dylan Mortenson. That, more than anything, revealed the pointlessness of his crush.

Em's best friends and bridesmaids trailed her, yacking away. Jasmine – she of the bouncy big boobs that had once mesmerised three school grades of teen boys – was partnering Digby, while Harry was paired with Teagan, a slim, heavily freckled redhead and former local who now lived interstate. Jas, like Em, he knew from school, but Teagan had been a year below and Harry wasn't as well-acquainted with her. What he did know was that her family had lost their farm the previous year in pretty dodgy circumstances, leading to some bad blood between them all.

From the smile on Teagan's face that drama was in the past. Then again, her happiness was probably thanks to the good-looking bloke she'd dragged down to Levenham with her. Lucas was protective of his turf, that's for sure. Last night, along with the bride's and groom's families, the wedding party had come together for a pub meal. Harry had only been trying to chat politely – Teagan was his partner, after all – but Lucas had thrown him such a fuck-off look that Harry had sought refuge with Em's Granny B. Not the smartest of moves. The old bird had eyed him up and down over the rim of her glass of Scotch, pursed her lipsticked mouth, and calmly asked whether he'd ever considered a fling with a lady of fine maturity. Harry had damn near spluttered his beer over the table in shock. Granny B had then roared with laughter and patted him patronisingly on the back, much to the amusement of the gathering and Harry's acute mortification.

He moved away from the window to where the boys were standing and shoved his hands back nervously into his pockets. He liked Josh a lot, which is why he was agreeing to this lunacy. That, and as groomsman he kind of had no choice. Harry was honoured to be asked anyway. It said a lot about their relationship and he hoped one day he might be able to demonstrate the same regard. They'd lost touch during Josh's time in Adelaide but on his return to Levenham last year, he and Harry had picked up where they left off, as if the gap was only a few months instead of years. Good mates were like that though. Now they caught up frequently. In the winter it was all football, thanks to their love for the hapless Gerrinton Giants, and in the summer they played basketball to keep fit and do something beyond work.

The women entered, chattering non-stop about dresses and the champagne they'd indulged in. All right for some. What Harry wouldn't do for a fortifying beer or two. Em kissed Josh fondly, while Harry received a smile and nod, but he noticed a distinct lack of warmth in the greeting Digby returned to his sister. Digby stepped toward Jas, effectively giving Em the shoulder. For a fleeting moment Em's mouth curved downward then returned to normal as Josh whispered something in her ear.

Harry frowned at Digby. Em's brother might be best man and Harry only groomsman, but that didn't mean

Harry was going to let anything spoil this wedding. And it wouldn't hurt Dig to set aside his blame for a few days. Em had nothing to do with Felicity's death other than the accident occurring on her property. The coroner had even found that her attempts to save Felicity had been as heroic as Josh's.

Jas seemed to have it under control though. The intense way she was talking to Dig, her body close, eye contact fierce and voice low, suggested a telling-off. It also implied intimacy. Interesting. He glanced at Teagan who was watching Dig and Jas also, her expression revealing she'd noticed the same. She met his gaze and for a moment they shared their private knowledge, before Em clapped her hands and drew their attention elsewhere.

"Ready?"

"Dig and I are," said Josh. "Harry's not. The big girl. He's terrified he's going to get waxed and lose all his manliness like Samson."

Harry rolled his eyes. Big girl, his arse. He was taller and more built than all of them put together. "At least I've got the testosterone to grow more."

"Stop fretting." A poke from Jas landed in his ribs. "They'll only wax you if you ask."

"I wasn't fretting."

"Sure, you weren't."

Fortunately, he was saved from more ribbing by the arrival of a short, slender woman with over-arched eyebrows, flawless skin and her blonde hair tied back in a bun. She looked like a doll. A doll with the greenest eyes he'd ever seen.

Harry couldn't stop staring. "Jesus," he muttered.

A nudge had him looking down. It was Teagan. "It's

all fake. Pancake makeup and coloured contact lenses."

"Right," he said, pursing his lips. He knew that.

"Everyone here?" asked Dollybird.

Em nodded. "And looking forward to it."

"Great. Everything's prepared." She smiled at them in turn. "Now, girls first." From the corridor behind emerged three equally slim women wearing outfits that seemed more appropriate for a pharmacy or science lab than a beauty salon. "Em, you're with Megan. Jas, if you'll go with Sandy? And Teagan, we've paired you with Katie."

Em planted a kiss on Josh's mouth before waving at Harry and Dig, and with a call of "Enjoy!" trailed her beautician down the corridor. Jas followed suit, throwing Dig a wink as she went.

Teagan touched Harry lightly on the arm. "Just relax. You'll be fine." Then she leaned close. "But if they offer you an enema, say no." And with a giggle she trotted off, leaving Harry feeling faint from the blood that had just drained from his face to pool in his boots. Enema? Enema?

Their hostess clasped her hands and smiled. "Now, for the boys. Josh, you're with Daniella, Digby you're with Madeline, and Harry, you're with our new arrival, Summer."

Harry shifted his attention from Dollybird to his beautician, who was stepping forward from behind the others. He blinked, and what little blood remained in his upper body rushed floorward.

He made a strangled noise, earning a startled look from Josh, before quickly covering it with a cough.

"You right there, big fella?"

"Yep, yep." He took a step back and turned, feigning more coughing while he calculated how much fallout there'd be if he legged it out of there. With an effort, Harry got a grip on himself. So what if his beautician was the girl from Gav's he'd given a mouthful to? He'd been in the right, and she'd deserved it. Mostly. Although he did feel a bit bad. A lot, when he'd let himself think about it. But she and her dumb horse had frightened the fuck out him that night. A bloke could be expected to get a bit loud.

Anyway, what harm could a tiny girl like her do? And he wasn't about to make a dick of himself in front of Josh and Dig. He'd never hear the bloody end of it.

Straightening his spine, he faced her again.

Summer's blue eyes were wide with recognition. When she'd stepped forward she'd been square-shouldered and smiling. Now the smile was gone and she seemed to have shrunk in on herself. She glanced across at Dollybird in a way that made Harry suddenly feel like the world's meanest bully, but Dollybird was already out from behind the counter and ushering Josh and Dig toward the corridor.

She paused alongside Summer, her tone and expression stern. Dollybird might possess a veneer of porcelain, but behind it she was hard as rock. "Everything all right?"

For a moment Summer didn't say anything. Then she visibly regathered herself – chin rising, fists curling at her sides, and a tough glint sparking in her slightly narrowed eyes.

"Yes. All fine." She regarded Harry with blank professionalism. "If you'll follow me?"

Swallowing, he nodded.

They walked in silence, both stiff with discomfort, but Harry sensed she somehow had the upper hand. This was her territory, after all, and he had no idea what was going to happen to him. He touched his palm to his shirt and rubbed anxiously. Surely she wouldn't wax his chest without permission, or sneak some de-hairing concoction on it? Harry rather liked his chest hair. An old girlfriend had once told him it was just right. Not too thick to be gorilla-ish, not too thin to be pathetic, but in enough abundance to be sexily appealing. Real man's chest hair.

Summer reached an open door and stepped aside, arm held out to indicate for him to enter. "Please remove your clothes down to your underwear. There's a towel on the bed to wrap around your waist. I'll return in a few minutes."

He peeked inside. The light was dim, flickering with lit candles arranged around the room, and giving off the tangy scent of orange or mandarin. The floor was pale timber, shelving and other fittings the same. In the centre sat a massage table with a pristine white toweling cover. A trolley on wheels was parked to one side at its end, trays filled with what looked like medicine bottles except with fancier labels.

Harry glanced at Summer, whose expression gave away nothing, except perhaps a little contempt. "Look, I can sit this out. Tell everyone I'm sick or something. Save us both the stress."

Her mouth twitched. "Are you afraid I'll hurt you?"

Hurt him? As if. Although he couldn't help another rub at his chest. That mouth twitch looked dangerous. This whole stupid thing was.

"Not at all. I just thought you might be, ah, uncomfortable with me after our, ah, chat."

"I'm a professional beautician and qualified masseuse, Mr. Argyle. I am perfectly capable of putting our chat" — she jerked a tight, insincere smile — "aside for our session."

"Yes, of course. I didn't mean to imply . . ."

"I'm sure." She gestured once more. "If you please? You'll find hangers for your clothes and a rack for your boots in the robe beside the basin."

With a final glance down the corridor, and a breath, Harry stepped inside. The door clicked shut softly behind him. He had to hand it to Summer, she had balls. In the same position he probably would have told him to stick his head up his arse.

He eyed the towel. Not a lot to cover himself with, but there was no turning back now. He'd just have to suck up whatever he had coming.

Five minutes later, when her knock came, he was standing at the edge of the bed with the inadequate towel around his hips and nerves making his mouth dry. He'd already used the tap to scoop water into his mouth, but the dryness refused to abate. He didn't want to guzzle too much in case it made him need the loo. Or burp. Or do anything to channel more of her contempt his way.

She entered, her professional mask in place. Her gaze flickered over his chest then away, and he resisted the urge to press his hand protectively there again. God knows what she could be scheming behind that indifference. Although, unlike Dollybird, Summer didn't seem to be wearing that much makeup, and while not as richly coloured, her blue eyes were definitely prettier. But he'd always been partial to blue-eyed brunettes. Probably why Maya had kept him hooked for so long. That and the fact she had legs like a giraffe.

His gaze dropped to Summer's lower half but her pharmacist's trousers were too baggy to reveal anything.

"If you're ready," she said with icy articulation, clearly having caught his inspection, "perhaps you could please take that seat over there." She pointed to the end of the room where a leather lounge chair was located, a thick bathmat in front. A low wooden tub of water, coopered like a half-barrel, was set to one side. "We'll start with a foot spa."

Some sort of plant material was floating in the tub, along with a few flowers. Harry peered at it, his nose screwing up a fraction. "Is that . . ."

"Cucumber. Yes. Along with some mint leaves and peppermint oil."

"Looks more like a cocktail than a foot spa."

"It's very soothing."

Sure it was. About as soothing as sticking your feet in an algae-filled cattle trough, but he sat down anyway.

Summer pulled the tub across and gently directed his feet into the cocktail mix. The bowl had a layer of smooth pebbles on the bottom. The water was warm, and the veg bumping into his ankles made Harry feel like he'd stuck his feet into a bowl of under-heated soup. Summer brought across a low wooden stool and a tray laden with creams and strange-looking tools, and settled down opposite him with a towel draped across her knees.

She stared at his feet, which, being big like the rest of him, took up most of the bowl. For want of anything else to do, Harry stared down too. He waited. And waited some more. But she continued to sit with her hands on her lap. Perhaps she was intimidated? Keeping his head low he raised his eyes to check on her, only to find her watching him in return.

"We're letting them soak a little. It'll help soften the excess skin."

"Oh. Okay."

He focused back on his feet, wishing he could think of something to say. Not sorry, but something to ease this awkward quiet, and the squirm of shame that had lodged inside him back in reception when she'd looked up and realised who her client was.

"Have you ever had a spa treatment before?" she asked.

"No."

"You'll enjoy it."

He caught her blue gaze and felt a flush creeping up his neck. He'd been too angry to pay much attention at Gav's but she really was very pretty, with a full mouth and a cute, slightly turned-up nose. The sort of girl that would cause his mum to kick him in the ankle and give one of her not very discreet, what-about-her nods. Despite her sons' protests, Harry's mum had never been backward in urging her offspring forward. She wanted grandkids, and Harry was going on thirty-one with not a girlfriend in sight.

He cleared his throat. "So, ah, Summer . . ."

She tilted her head and blinked slowly. Her lashes were long and thick and Harry felt a weird urge to touch them, or better still, have them flutter against his cheek. He dropped his focus back to his feet. Jesus, where had that come from?

"Yes?"

"Ah. Um." Christ, now he was stuttering. He breathed in and looked up. "Dollybird said that . . ." Her eyebrows lifted. Shit. "I mean, ah, the sheila at the counter." He frowned. That hadn't come out right either. And since when did he call anyone "sheila"? The word made him sound like his grandpa. Harry cleared his throat and tried again. "Your boss?"

"Grace, you mean?"

"Yeah. Grace." His fingers dug into the granite muscles of his thighs. Man, he was tense. "She said you were new?"

"I am."

He waited for her to elaborate but clearly Summer wasn't going to make this easy for him. "New to Levenham?" He cringed at yet another rising inflection. Now he sounded not only like a dick, but a girl, too.

"Yes."

"Okay." Harry nodded and shifted his attention around the room, pretending he didn't mind that she'd effectively told him to fuck off.

Summer bent forward, lowering her hand into the water. She lifted up his left foot and held it cupped in one palm while she began to massage the balls of his feet using one of the pebbles. If he wasn't feeling so edgy he would have groaned at the touch.

Harry stared at his foot and the delicate hands that stroked it. He'd never been embarrassed by his feet before, but against her fine bones they seemed clumsy and huge. And white from wearing boots all day. His lifted leg seemed ugly too – thick with coarse hairs, when he could barely see the hairs on her arms. Of those that existed he bet they were soft, like her caress. She had the silkiest hands he'd ever encountered and they were on his callused feet, of all places.

She looked up. "Am I hurting you?"

"No." He shook his head, staring at the tiny hand cupping his instep, the other poised with the stone, and felt completely discombobulated. "Not at all."

"Ticklish?"

"Not usually."

She resumed her massage. "Just say if you feel uncomfortable. The purpose of today is to relax."

"Bit hard after, ah, you know."

"I'll consider it a challenge. A test of my skill."

"Right. Good."

A faint curl of a smile edged her mouth but she said nothing.

An application of grit-filled gel stuff followed – exfoliating scrub, Summer explained – and was vigorously rubbed into his feet and then rinsed away. She used tools to smooth some of the hard skin, her cheeks glowing sweetly from the effort. By the time the treatment was complete, his feet were tingling with cleanliness. Even his toenails were pink, white and shiny.

"There," she said, lowering his towel-dried left foot to the mat and rising from the stool. "All done. Feel nice?"

"Yeah. It does." Very nice. Like he'd been given new feet.

"Now you get to enjoy the really good part."

"I do?"

"You do." Summer indicated the massage table. "When you're ready, if you could lie on the table for me, face down, we'll start with the fully body massage and then end with a facial."

"Facial?"

"Yes. Like what I did with your feet, except for your face and neck."

"Okay." He stood, hesitating. "No waxing?"

Summer had crouched to gather her tools but at the mention of waxing she straightened. The contempt that had seemed to dissipate while she'd worked on his feet was back. She spoke in a clipped, robotic manner that threw him even more off-guard.

"If you desire. However, I must advise right now it's not salon policy to wax men's genital region. You'll have to find another salon. I believe Christiane's on Davis Street does it."

"Geni– What?" Then it clicked. His palms shot up. "No, no. That's not what I meant. I don't want anything waxed, especially not . . ." He couldn't even bring himself to say it. Even the thought was causing his balls to shrink up inside his body. "I just wanted to make sure that wasn't part of the process."

"Oh. No, of course it isn't. Not unless you'd like it to be." She resumed cleaning up. "Some men do have their chests and backs waxed for aesthetic reasons. Or their eyebrows shaped."

"Girls," muttered Harry.

Summer heard and chuckled, and regarded him with amusement. "You're not very new-age sensitive, are you?"

"I am." He set his jaw. "Just because I don't want my eyebrows or anything else waxed doesn't mean I can't be sensitive. If you must know, I'm renowned for it." He was too. With his giant's build he might not look it, but inside he was a big softie. Both the Argyle boys were.

Their mum had made sure of that.

For some reason the declaration only made her amusement wilt. Harry rubbed his neck, scrutinising Summer as she turned stiffly away, wondering what he'd said wrong.

He stood for a moment, confounded, then shrugged and lowered himself onto the table. It was comfortable, firm but sort of squishy. Where a pillow would normally be, there was a hole for his face. With a last glance Summer's way, he sank his head into it and stared at the grain of the timber floor.

A few seconds passed. Then a minute. Harry strained to hear what she was up to. Bottles clinked, then she padded across the floor. Music began to filter through the room. A flowing kind of electronica he found surprisingly tuneful. Quiet steps sounded again. Another rattle followed by a strong waft of citrus. Then a startling trickle of liquid on his back caused his head to jerk up.

A hand pressed on his shoulder. "Relax."

"What was that?"

"Just oil. Now put your head back down and concentrate on taking slow, even breaths."

He did as he was told but the tension remained.

More oil dribbled over his skin. He twitched, his nervousness back in full. Which was ridiculous. He'd had remedial massages before for footy aches and pains, but this was very different. With the music and candlelight, the moment seemed almost intimate.

Oil was pooling along his spine like sweat. Harry itched to rub it off or roll to let it slide elsewhere. The massage seemed to be a long time coming but he wasn't about to show more weakness and lift his head again.

Finally, just as Harry thought he was going to start breaking out in involuntary tics, smooth warm hands closed over his back and began sliding with easy efficiency over his skin.

At first the weird closeness of it made him hunch. This was what lovers did in bed for pleasure and fun. Not the sort of thing a decent man paid for. The way his mind was working didn't help either. With only the floor to amuse him, Harry couldn't stop thinking of the look Summer had thrown Dollybird. Sure, she'd recovered quickly but the despair he'd seen – or was it fear? – kept churning in his guts. That wasn't him. He wasn't the kind of bloke to make a woman feel that way. Yet clearly, he had.

And the thought made him feel ashamed.

As she smoothed and kneaded and stroked, he replayed the night he'd yelled at her. He hadn't meant to but she'd frightened the shit out of him. Not only had he nearly collided with her horse, he'd come damn close to skittling her. When the car finally stopped and he saw her on her knees, the horrible lurch in his guts had made him think he had hit her. The ensuing temper was simply him venting that fright, and his frustration over old Gav. Hardly an unusual reaction. Lots of people reacted that way after having the bejesus scared out of them.

Didn't they?

Except the more he mulled the more he began to reassess, and consider the event as Summer might have. A big bloke – and by anyone's standards Harry was huge – towering over her in the dark and bellowing like a bull? No wonder she'd reacted the way she had when she saw him. The poor girl likely thought he was back for round two.

No two ways about it, he'd have to apologise. Right now.

Harry lifted his head. "Listen, Summer, about the other night."

She paused, and continued to knead the flesh around his waist and the hollow at the base of his spine. "You're meant to be relaxing."

"I can't. Not until I say sorry. I shouldn't have yelled at you. That was wrong."

The pressure lessened. He twisted to look at her face. She was standing by the table with her hands by her side, her bottom lip sucked in.

"I'm sorry. I mean it."

Her gaze moved to his and for a long moment she simply stared, then she nodded.

Harry waited for more but it appeared a nod was all he was going to get. Fair enough. It was probably all he deserved. He buried his face back into the table's hollow, feeling like shit.

There was an extended hiatus before she continued her massage, then her hands were back working his muscles and skin. Perhaps it was wishful thinking on his part, but they seemed gentler now, her kneading smoother.

"You're not relaxing," she said after a while.

"Sorry."

"You're not helping my professional pride, you know."

Harry smiled at that. "I'll try."

She moved further up his back to concentrate on his left shoulder and arm, stretching it out and massaging from the tips of his fingers, right up the length of his arm, to the end of his collarbone. "Will it help if I change the music?"

"Nah, it's okay." And it was. Now that he had his apology out of the way Harry felt much better. The way she worked his hand, thumbs circling the centre of his palm, felt good. Really good.

Slowly, as she moved from one arm to the other, Harry truly did begin to relax. His body began to get heavy, his chest and hips sinking further and further into the soft mattress. His brain began to switch to that vagued-out dreamy state like just before sleep. The scented air smelled sweet, further dulling his mind. He began to drift on a serene wave of pleasure, savouring the smooth strength of her touch. The satin feel of her hands. The rhythm of the music adding to his feeling of contented well-being.

He was, as she'd promised, beginning to enjoy this. A lot.

Then she moved to his legs.

THREE

Harry proved such a long lump of a man that his legs extended well over the end of the table. His broad back and muscular shoulders nearly filled its width too. Summer had massaged a few sportsmen in her time but never one quite so ... She wasn't sure how to describe him. He wasn't body-builder muscular, or like the super-fit who were so lacking in body fat, all she felt was bone, muscle and sinew. He was simply tall and, well, rather deliciously meaty.

He smelled nice too. Often the men who came in for treatments overdid it with the cologne or deodorant. Harry just smelled clean, with a hint of spice. Not that any of that had any bearing on the way Summer felt about him. Good-looking lump or not, he was still a thug.

But she'd been in this business one way or another since she'd left school and she knew how to maintain professional detachment. Except for the little hiccup when she'd first caught sight of him at reception, and again when she'd seen him standing bare-chested by the table, she'd been fine. He was the one naked, after all. And to her delight he'd been even more stupid with nerves than her. Stuttering and making a fool of himself. The schoolgirl in her had cheered, but as his little-boy-lost bumbling continued, the woman in her had begun to feel a tiny bit sorry for him.

Then he'd gone and ruined it by claiming he was sensitive. Yeah, sure he was. So sensitive he thought it perfectly acceptable to insult and swear at a woman half his size, then menace and threaten her like a mafia hit man. Worst of all, he'd called poor innocent Binky stupid.

If anyone was stupid it was Harry Argyle.

Determined not to be charmed by his looks, muscle and little boy act, Summer had held onto that mean thought while she'd worked. Which made his apology, when it came, highly annoying. He'd sounded genuinely contrite.

She hadn't expected that. It certainly hadn't seemed on the cards in the beginning when he'd patronisingly referred to their altercation as a chat. A foot soak and a few rubs later and it was as if something suddenly clicked in his Neanderthal brain, and he'd realised how truly awful he'd been to her.

Men were curious creatures. This one in particular.

Didn't mean she forgave him though.

Summer focused on working his calves. They were solid; the sort of calves you'd see in a man who walked a lot or ran. The tan line amused her. A definite ring at sock height that made his feet look like they'd been dipped in pale pink paint. The hair had been worn away a bit there too. Same on his calves. Where his jeans rubbed, she supposed.

She kneaded her way up to his knee and the bottom of his thigh and immediately felt him stiffen. The muscles flexed and tension tightened his hamstring. She glanced at his upper body. His face remained buried but his shoulders were hunched up near his ears. Not a good

44

sign.

"Is it too hard?"

He didn't answer straight away. Finally a strangled "no" emerged. Summer frowned and softened her touch anyway. She'd been firm. Men usually enjoyed a deeper massage, and even if they didn't, masculine pride prevented them from complaining. She could always feel it though, and would ease off accordingly. Summer was trained in various forms of massage therapy but not remedial, which was specialised. Her treatments were about pleasure, not pain.

Even with a lighter touch he remained tense. Summer kept frowning at his back, undecided whether to ask what the problem was. He didn't seem the type to complain to the boss, but you never knew with people. Clients could be all smiles, swearing they'd had a wonderful session, only to phone in the next day whinging about anything from the temperature of the massage oil to the music, or that her hair wasn't neat enough. A few years ago, she'd even had a client moan that the squeak of Summer's soft-soled shoes had completely ruined the ambience of the room and consequently their experience. Fortunately her boss at the time was a veteran, and after making the usual apologies and offering a discount off the client's next session, had hung up with an eye roll, and a don't-worry-about-it smile and pat on the shoulder.

Summer suspected her new boss, Grace, who was younger than her, definitely less experienced, and prone to jealousy, wouldn't be so understanding. And she needed this job, badly.

The worry had her taking even more care with Harry. She smoothed her hands up and down his legs, using extra oil and concentrating on making the massage as agreeable as possible. Yet it seemed the more she worked, the more tense he became, and the more worried she felt.

In despair she gave up, and asked him to roll over.

"It's okay," he said, not moving his head from its cradle. "I'll just lay here for a minute."

"Mr. Argyle."

His face finally appeared. "Harry. You can call me Harry." He gave a weird kind of smile then buried his head again.

She stared at the short dark hair of the back of his skull, at a loss. "I think it's best if we keep this professional, don't you?"

"Mmph."

Which about summed up her sentiments too. Calling him Mr. Argyle was ridiculous, and not something she normally did, especially with someone of her own generation. She'd started with the mister thing as a kind of sly insult, just to let him know where they stood with one another. But now it was making Summer look foolish and would do nothing to get him onside.

"Look, Harry," she said, moving to his side where they could see each other properly. "I really need you to roll over."

Another head lift, another crazy smile. "We've probably done enough, yeah?"

Sweat began to break down Summer's spine. The man was a nightmare. "We've still another hour and a half to go. Thirty minutes more of massage, then an hour-long facial. It's part of the package."

"I'll just sleep." He nodded, as if that sounded the best idea in the world. "Yeah. That'll do. You can go out for coffee or something."

"You can't!" She swallowed and took several long breaths. "Is it something I've done? Are you in pain? A cramp, perhaps?" She took a step toward his legs. "I could help."

"No!" This time it was his turn to swallow and take breaths. "It's fine. You haven't hurt me and I don't have cramp, okay?"

"Then what?"

Harry stared fixedly at the wall.

"Oh," she said, placing her palm to her forehead. "I see. You've . . ." She waggled a finger at his bum, then snapped it to her side when she clocked Harry's expression.

Humiliation had turned his cheeks scarlet. His eyes were closed, as if praying for his problem to go away, or for her to. Or perhaps he was doing maths equations or going over sports statistics or whatever it was that men did in these situations.

Plastering a professional smile on her face, when all she really wanted to do was bounce and giggle in vengeful glee, Summer rested a hand on his shoulder and tried to catch his gaze. "You don't have to be embarrassed. You'd be surprised how often it happens."

Though he opened his eyes, he refused to look at her.

"Look, I've been doing this a long time and I've seen pretty much everything. A little erection isn't going to bother me, okay?"

His eyebrows shot up and this time she couldn't help her laughter.

"Sorry, bad choice of words." She gave him a pat that was more an admonishing light smack. "Now stop acting like a teenager and roll over."

"Don't want to."

"Harry, if I don't finish this properly I'll get into trouble. I can't afford that. This is the only dedicated spa in town. The rest are normal salons attached to hairdressers and the like, and they only employ one or two people. If I lose this job I'd struggle to get another, and I really don't want to have to move again. So, please, if you honestly want to make up for yelling at me and Binky, then roll over."

His slump of defeat told her she'd won. With one hand over his nethers, Harry began to shuffle onto his back. His mouth a thin line, he stared fixedly at the ceiling, both hands attempting to hide the evidence of his arousal. Summer did her best to not look anywhere below his waist but she found her gaze flicking there regardless. From the way the towel and his hands were angled, there was clearly nothing little about this erection.

It appeared Harry was a big man in every way.

The thought had her almost giggling again but she suppressed it. "I won't do your legs, how's that? We'll just focus on your upper body and give you an extra long facial."

"'Kay."

She smiled at him. "That also means you're going to have to take your hands away and put them by your side."

His chest heaved with the breath he took. His mouth thinned even further, but slowly, he obeyed. Summer pretended to hunt for a product on her tray, commanding herself not to look. But she was a red-blooded woman and it was impossible not to gawk. That earlier peek really didn't seem enough.

She glanced, then to her shame, downright ogled. He wasn't just big, he was huge.

His hands shot back to the towel. "I thought you said it wouldn't bother you."

"I . . ."

Harry swung his legs over the edge and sat up, hands gripping the table like he was in danger of falling off. His head was down but Summer could see his jaw was flexed. Angry, most likely, as was warranted. She'd really overstepped the mark. Her heart began to thud in panic. If she lost her job, she'd couldn't afford to pay rent or agistment. Then where would she and Binky go? Home to Haikenvale? She loved her family but beauty therapy was her calling. She could start her own business but, as had been proven to her detriment, the village was simply too tiny to sustain a full-time clinic.

She stepped back, the bottle of massage oil held protectively at her chest, feeling slightly wild. "I'm sorry."

He looked up. "You don't have to be sorry. I'm the one with a . . ." He turned his face, jaw tightening again. "You know."

"Yes, but I stared and embarrassed you. That was grossly unprofessional."

"I should go," he said, sliding to his feet.

"No, please don't." Summer threw a panicked look at the door. No matter what excuse he used she'd get the blame, she knew it. "We'll . . ." She cast around frantically, trying to think of another treatment but her mind wasn't functioning. To Summer's horror her throat began to thicken and turn gravelly, a sure sign tears were on their way. She swallowed hard but her voice still came out husky and small. "Can't we at least do the facial?"

"Hey." He stepped toward her and placed a hand on her arm. His brown gaze was soft with concern. "What's up?" He smiled wryly. "Besides me."

She blinked and breathed through her nose, forcing the tears away. "I don't want to get into trouble."

"You won't. I'll say I'm sick. Don't worry about the money. I'll cover the full fee."

"She'll still blame me."

"Dollybird? I won't let her. Did you know her eye colour's fake? Contact lenses."

"Yes."

He leaned down and inspected her eyes. "You don't wear them, do you?"

"Yes, but not coloured ones. I'm a bit short-sighted."

"Thought yours were real. They're much prettier than her fake ones."

Summer tried to smile at the compliment but it emerged wobbly. This talk was all very nice but he was still standing, ready to leave. She let out a resigned sigh. "I'm very sorry this has been uncomfortable for you. I never meant it to be that way. I'll leave you to get dressed."

"Actually," said Harry, suddenly grinning, "I've changed my mind. Looks like the problem's solved itself."

They both looked down and up again. Summer slapped her hand over her mouth to stop herself giggling. Harry began to laugh. It was a pleasant man's laugh, deep and honest, the sort you'd like to hear a lot.

He tilted his head toward the table. "Guess I'd better get back on the horse."

As he turned she caught his hand and gave it a meaningful squeeze. "Thank you."

The smile he gave her was dazzling. "You're welcome, Summer."

***

The stink hit her the moment she opened the door.

Summer stepped back a few paces, inhaled deeply, then cupped her palm over her mouth and nose and pushed into the kitchen. Dismay settled on her shoulders, and worry.

Gav's sink was piled with unwashed dishes. Mugs mostly, and cheap glasses. Crusts from what looked like a toasted sandwich were still sitting on a small plate. A fly probed the semi-dried smear of tomato sauce on its surface.

Summer swallowed as the house remained quiet and fear began to creep inside her. She hovered, staring at the hallway entrance. Gav had been on a bender, a big one. She could tell by the smell: vomit, urine laced with spilled alcohol. And silence.

"Gav?"

Nothing. God, she hoped he was sleeping it off. Anything else was too horrifying.

She took a hesitant step toward the hall. The first door on the right was the lounge. Best case scenario, she'd find him racked out on the couch. Worst . . .

She shook the thought off. Gav would be fine. Drunk, no doubt, three-quarters along the way to killing himself, but alive. She dropped her hand from her mouth. The stink was less overpowering now she'd grown used to it. Once she'd sorted Gav, she needed to track down where he'd made his messes and clean them up. It wasn't her job, but since she was the enabler – the one who'd given him the funds to go on this drinking spree – guilt dictated she should.

"Gav?" Still nothing.

Stiffening her back, Summer headed into the living room.

The television was on but the sound muted. Two empty spirit bottles were stacked at the side of the ragged two-seater couch, strangely neat against the rest of the room's disarray. A dark stain covered the cushion of one side of the couch, perhaps new, perhaps old. Summer wasn't about to touch it to find out if it was still damp. The television's remote had been plonked head first into yet another dirty glass. She picked it up and turned the television off, then paused to listen. Only creaks. Not even a snore. Surely she would hear something?

Rising alarm set her heart whumping. She strode out of the living room, pulling her mobile phone from her jeans pocket as she did. The door to a spare bedroom stood open off the hall; Summer poked her head in, quickly scanned and kept going.

"Gav!"

The bathroom and toilet were next. They were empty, but she discovered the source of the vomit stench. Perhaps the urine too, given the large wet patch near the vanity. The steel towel rail drooped toward the floor where one end had been wrenched from the wall. Gav had probably grabbed it in an attempt to keep himself upright. Her grandfather had once done the same. It was amazing the damage a drunk could do, to their homes as well as themselves. Summer's poppy had once sheared the entire lip of a tile soap dish from the wall, snapping it like a cracker biscuit. Glue had fixed that. Poppy's hand had required several stitches.

At least there was no blood in the bathroom. But that didn't mean Gav wasn't lying somewhere, hurt.

She called his name again as she strode the last few steps to his bedroom, she assumed. No one answered.

Drawn blinds kept the room in darkness. Summer found the light switch and flicked it on and off but the bulb remained dead. She blinked, trying to adjust her eyes but she could already see the bed was rumpled, but empty. It should have left her relieved, except it didn't. If Gav wasn't in the house, where the hell was he?

She walked to the other side of the bed just to check he hadn't fallen out and was lying hurt on the floor. Tapping her phone against the end of her curled fist, she bit her lip and tried to think of where a drunk might go. Or try to. Two seconds later she broke into a run.

The driver's door of Gav's ute was open. Feet were sticking out, one with a boot, the other with only a sock. The other boot lay on the dirt floor of the carport where it had been pulled off and discarded, or had fallen from never being on properly in the first place. Gav was tilted sideways over the seats, facing the dash. His eyes were closed. Something whitish and flaky had dried around one corner of his mouth. From the colour of his trousers he'd had another accident.

Summer grabbed his legs and shook. "Gav! Gav!"

She tried to drag him toward her but even with his undernourished body he was too heavy. She'd never be able to lift him out without assistance, and even she understood that dragging a potentially sick or injured man to the ground was unwise. Summer raced to the passenger door and swung it open. Kneeling on the edge of the seat she touched his face, calling to him. He was cool but not cold. She felt under his nostrils but panic made her uncertain if there was breath, or only her wishful thinking. A touch of his neck elicited no sign of a pulse, but that didn't mean anything. Summer had no first aid experience or training. What she did have was a phone.

She kept touching Gav's face as she talked to the emergency operator, wanting to cry but aware now wasn't the time. Gav needed help. Self-indulgent tears could come later.

The operator kept talking to her, asking questions about Gav. Summer did her best to answer, all the while keeping her ear out for the ambulance, and occasionally whispering to Gav, pleading with him to be all right. He wasn't a bad man, just a lonely one, whose only refuge from his solitary life and grief was alcohol. Her poppy had been the same, except in his case it wasn't a wife he mourned, but a son. Summer's uncle and her father's elder brother. The chosen one, as her dad once bitterly called him when they discovered Poppy after one of his benders. She hadn't blamed her dad for that either. It was simply a manifestation of the frustration they all felt. The dead were gone, the living still existed. Yet these men acted as though death held them in a stranglehold.

A car sounded from the road. She stroked Gav's thin lank hair. "I'll be right back." She ran to the end of the drive, ready to wave the ambulance over, but it wasn't the ambulance. A plain white tray-top ute, its indicator on, was traveling slowly down the gravel road, as though looking to turn in to Binky's paddock. The driver spotted her, accelerated for the main drive before pulling off the road on to the verge.

It was Harry Argyle, and if he was here to tell her off again he would discover the true capacity of her own temper. To her relief he didn't seem mad. Instead he wore a shy, almost embarrassed smile, which lasted about as long as it took for him to focus properly on her expression.

"Summer?"

She pointed back up the drive toward the carport. "It's Gav."

Harry didn't hesitate. He broke into a jog, leaving Summer to follow. She turned to do so but the sound of another engine kept her rooted. Seconds later the ambulance crested the hill. She stepped out and waved. Confident they'd seen her, she ran back up the drive.

Harry was bent inside the passenger side of the ute. To Summer's untrained eye, he seemed to know what he was doing. He was talking to Gav, asking if he could hear him. One set of fingers was pressed against Gav's throat while the others were prising open his mouth.

"The paramedics are here," said Summer, wringing her hands.

"Good." Harry slid out of the car to make room and greeted the first paramedic. "Tommo."

"Harry, how are you?"

"Not bad." He indicated Gav. "He's breathing."

Tommo nodded. "Drunk?"

"Looks like it. Could be something else though."

"You find him?"

"No. Summer did."

"I think he might have run out of booze and tried to get into town to buy more," said Summer. "There are a couple of empty Scotch bottles inside."

"Right-o," said Tommo, sounding unsurprised and leaving Summer to wonder if this wasn't the first time he'd been called here. Poor Gav. Why hadn't anyone tried to help him? She stopped herself. No doubt someone had, but if Gav was anything like her poppy, he'd probably refused all assistance.

Harry greeted the other paramedic and moved well out of the way, indicating for Summer to join him.

"Do you think he'll be all right?" she asked.

"Yeah." His expression turned grim. "Once he sobers up. What about you? You must have had a hell of a fright."

She crossed her arms and cupped her elbows, staring at the ute. "I'm just scared for him."

"I'm sure he'll be all right. Gav's a tough old bugger."

She shook her head. "He's not. I've seen it before. He's been like this too long. There's no way out now." She dug her teeth into her lip to stifle a sob. "This is my fault."

"Hey, hey." Harry wrapped an arm around her. It felt solid and comforting. "It's not."

"It is. I gave him the money." A tear began to leak down her cheek. "I've been trying to help, bringing him meals, making sure he's feeding himself, washing. Trying to keep him human, you know?"

Harry nodded.

"But any good I do is destroyed the moment I hand over Binky's agistment fee. I know damn well what he's going to do with the money and it makes me sick every time. But I don't know what else to do. I can't not pay him. God!" She touched her fingers to her forehead and closed her eyes. "I should have checked on him. But we had three weddings on the weekend that I had to do makeup for and I was so tired. I should have at least poked my head in when I came to feed Binky. Except I didn't. Because deep down I knew what I'd find and I just didn't want to face it." She took a shuddery breath and sniffed, then stepped out from under Harry's arm to wipe at her eyes. "What are you doing here anyway?"

She hadn't seen him since the wedding party's group appointment the previous Friday, four days ago. Summer had spent the days since expecting a bawling out or worse from Grace, but there'd been nothing. Harry's session had ended positively, or so she'd hoped, but you never knew, and her own unprofessionalism still sat uneasily with her. It had taken her until lunchtime on Tuesday to accept she was in the clear.

"Just passing. Saw your car. Thought I'd, ah" – he scratched at the back of his head – "say hello. And thanks. You know, for the other day. It was good, despite the, um . . ." He winced as though the memory hurt.

"I'm glad you enjoyed it."

"I did. A lot. The others did too. Josh reckons he's going to have another go."

"What about you?"

His cheeks reddened and he used the toe of one boot to scratch at the calf of the other leg. "Nah. I've already made a big enough dick –" He closed his eyes. "Shit."

If she weren't feeling so ill over Gav, Summer might have made a teasing comment. Instead she offered a sympathetic smile and refocused on the paramedics who were easing him out onto a stretcher. Summer inhaled sharply as Gav made a moaning noise, and hurried over.

She hovered, not wanting to get in the way but desperate to let him know she was there, that he wasn't alone.

"Will he be all right?"

"We'll get him to the hospital," said Tommo. "Let the doctors do their thing."

Summer rolled her lips together at the non-answer, then looked up as Harry positioned his bulk alongside her.

"He'll be fine."

She nodded, although she wasn't confident. Though Gav was moaning, his eyes were still closed. He could have had a stroke, or heart attack. There could be brain damage. Anything. No one drank that much booze without causing harm.

"I'll need to lock up. Find his car keys." She glanced to where her horse stood at the fence, watching them with twitching ears. "And feed Binky."

"I'll help."

"You don't have to. I'll be all right. I'm sure you have other things to do."

"The quicker you get it done, the quicker you can get to the hospital." He smiled a little. "Besides, I have things to make up for."

"All that doesn't matter."

"Yeah, Summer," he said, holding her gaze. "It does."

His words made something balloon in her chest before it was popped by another moan from Gav. The paramedics had him lifted and were walking toward the ambulance. Summer followed, wanting to take Gav's hand but he was wrapped up snug.

"I'm here, Gav. You're going to be fine. They're taking you to the hospital. I'll see you there, okay?"

She had no idea if he'd heard her but she hoped he had. Someone had to be on his side. Once he came round and everyone started on him, he'd feel more alone than ever. Her poppy once told her that getting lectured by a nurse less than half his age had made him wish he'd taken one of the farm's rifles and shot himself instead. She'd pleaded with him to not think that way, but his illness had dug claws into his heart and mind, and he'd meant every word. When Summer told her parents what he'd said, they'd confiscated the guns. It hadn't made any difference. The next bender proved too much for Poppy's weakened body anyway and he got his wish.

If only she could stop Gav from getting his.

FOUR

Scavenging through a reeking house with an increasingly fretful Summer, was not how Harry had planned for this to go. If that old bastard Gav wasn't sick and on his way to hospital, Harry would have brained him one.

It had taken them fifteen minutes to track down the keys to Gav's ute, which were, much to Harry's disgust, hidden in the sink under the flyblown dishes. He'd rinsed them off, then helped Summer quickly scoop up and sluice down the worst of the bathroom mess, before closing up the house and locking the ute. All the time she'd remained quiet. He hoped it wasn't guilt silencing her but he had a nasty feeling it was.

Another reason Gav deserved a good smack.

"Back up, Bobby," he told the horse as he held fence wires apart for Summer.

"Binky."

"Oh. Sorry." Harry eyed her backside as she climbed through, wishing she was wearing jodhpurs like the other day. He'd been enjoying a few sexy daydreams about her in riding gear, and jeans didn't show off her assets nearly as well. "Funny name."

"Short for Mister Binks." She straightened and nodded. "Thanks."

"What can I do?"

"Nothing. You don't have to do anything. I can manage."

Harry rubbed the back of his neck, thinking. A perfunctory dismissal after cleaning up sick and God knows what else wasn't part of his seduction strategy. The way he'd pictured it, he was to drive casually down the road, spot Summer's car and pull up to say g'day. It would just so happen he'd have a couple of apples on the passenger seat, which he'd offer to her horse, much to her appreciation. That would lead to a bit more conversation. Then he'd slip in something about maybe going out for a drink one night, to say thanks for the massage and sorry for yelling at her, getting a hard-on, generally being an idiot . . .

Not going to happen now. Fuck it. Which left him at a loss.

Summer nudged Binky aside, turned off the electric fence and began to unroll the tarp covering a small stack of hay. Realising he was just standing there like a dork, Harry rushed to help.

"Honestly, Harry, I'm just about done. And as soon as I am I'm going to the hospital."

"Do you want me to come with you?"

She paused, the biscuits of hay she was separating from the bale half open like fanned book leaves, and studied him for a long moment, a small furrow between her brows. Harry didn't like the look of that. Offering to go to the hospital must have been one step too far.

But what was he meant to do? He hadn't been able to stop thinking about her since Friday. Half of him wanted to hide in shame, the other half was so excited he was struggling to contain it. Even though it was the long way round, he'd taken the gravel road to town and back every trip. Not to mooch over Maya, as he usually did, but in the faint hope he'd see Summer. On Monday, during their suit fitting, he'd been so distracted that Josh had teased that Harry must be in love. Which he wasn't. Well, not much.

It wasn't all about the massage and the way she'd made him feel – which was pretty damn good, not to mention as toey as a Roman sandal – but how she'd reacted to his embarrassment. Summer was sweet, a bit playful, and nicer than he deserved, even though he'd managed to stick his boot in it and upset her again. The list of things he needed to make up for seemed to grow with every encounter.

And from the way she was looking at him now, he was on the cusp of adding another to it.

"Thanks for the offer," she said, concentrating back on the hay, "but that won't be necessary."

"Okay. No problem." Harry scratched at his nose, looked back to the house, then at Binky, then Summer, who'd gathered the biscuits and was waiting for him to do something. Hint taken, he gestured dumbly toward the road. "I'll be off then."

"Thanks for your help with Gav."

He nodded and went to step away, but hesitated. A few words, that's all he needed. A bit of a "How about a drink sometime?" People asked each other out every day. It was normal. Except Summer wasn't exactly acting receptive, and he wasn't sure he'd even come close to making up for yelling at her. She probably thought he was being a creepy stalker.

His fingers twitched. To ask or not to ask?

Summer tilted her head, eyebrows drawn.

Definitely not then.

"Right. I'll, ah, see you."

He could feel her gaze on him the entire way down the paddock to the gate. Or he thought he could. When he glanced back, Summer was busy with her horse. Harry smiled wryly and shook his head. Another woman, another unreciprocated crush.

Situation bloody normal.

***

Thursday night was the wedding rehearsal. These things, Harry decided, were mainly for the bride and bridesmaids, who had to do the full aisle parade and generally make sure the bride didn't trip over her train, ruin her makeup from bawling, or turn into Bridezilla half-way through. All he, Dig and Josh had to do was stand around, hand over rings or whatever, pull faces at the flower girl and page boy, and walk the girls back down the aisle without making twits of themselves.

Although Josh did have to remember his "I do". Important bit that.

As Harry did the final slow walk with Teagan on his arm he could feel her scrutinising him sideways. Fortunately this time round her boyfriend was parked in the pub, waiting for them to finish, and Harry felt less self-conscious about talking to her.

"You're a woman," he said, after several seconds trying to think how to broach the subject, and clearing his throat.

"I know this will probably come as a shock to you,

Harry, but yes, I am."

"What? Oh." He grinned. "Sorry. Didn't mean it like that. I mean, you must think like one." Crap. That didn't come out right either. Now Teagan was all but laughing at him. He stared sulkily at Jasmine's back. No wonder he didn't have a girlfriend. They all thought he was an idiot. Which he was. "Forget it."

"Sorry. Can't now."

"Girl problems, Harry?" said Jas over her shoulder, clearly having listened in.

"Does Harry have girl problems?" This time it was Em. The entire wedding party ground to a halt in the centre of the aisle and turned as one to look at him.

Harry raised his eyes to the arched ceiling. Man, he was dumb. It was a big old airy church, built in the 1850s. Every word probably echoed. When he looked back down, he caught Josh nudging Em.

"Harry suffered a little" – Josh placed special emphasis on the word little – "problem with his beautician at the spa on Friday that he wants to make up for."

Em looked from Josh to Harry. "What problem? They've always been very good there. Gran goes all the time."

"Nothing," said Harry, gritting his teeth and throwing Josh a "prepare to die" glower. "Just forget it."

Teagan nudged him. "Come on. Spit it out."

"No." He shot Josh – who was grinning hugely at Harry's discomfort – another glare. The only person who seemed to be sympathetic was Digby.

"Is it Maya?" said Jas. "Because you probably should know she's seeing Dylan Mortenson."

Harry's teeth were beginning to ache from the pressure he was putting on them. "I know that."

"Then what?" asked Em, looking from Josh to Harry and back again. She folded her arms, her expression fixed and her tone turning coolly articulate in that haughty way she sometimes summoned, which Josh reckoned he found a huge turn-on and Harry found slightly terrifying. "If there's a problem, I need to know. Josh mentioned how impressed you were with Summer so I booked her for Saturday to help with makeup."

Harry was so delighted by the news he forgot himself. "You did?"

The entire group let out an "ah".

Both Em and Teagan covered their mouths to hide their grins. Jas simply laughed outright.

Harry puffed out a breath and stared at the carpet. He hadn't seen Summer since Tuesday, despite having driven past Gav's several times. According to his mum – the font of all local news – Gav was still in hospital. Harry had been tempted to take the old bugger a bottle of ginger ale on the off chance he might run into Summer at his bedside.

Digby came to his rescue. "Can this wait? I don't know about you, but I could do with a beer. And Lucas is stuck in the pub by himself."

Harry gave him a grimace of thanks but he knew the respite wouldn't be for long. As soon as they were settled in the back bar of the Australian Arms, the girls would start up again.

And start they did, wheedling out the story of Harry's encounters with Binky and Gav's fence, how he'd yelled at Summer in fright after he nearly skittled her, his dorkish apology at the spa, and efforts since to make it up to her. He left the bit out about the embarrassing massage. A sly warning to Josh about not wanting a black eye for Saturday kept his mate's gob shut too, though he could tell buy the secretive curve to Em's mouth that he'd told her what had happened.

Although knowing that also made him wistful. It must be nice to share stuff with someone, to talk and share secrets.

"So what are you going to do about it?"

He concentrated back on Jas who, Teagan had earlier warned, was high as a kite on Digby-sex and wedding fever, and in the mood for matchmaking.

"Take her apples for Binky?"

A statement that was received with laughter, quickly muffled when they realised he was serious.

"You're such a nong," said Jas. "No wonder you're single."

"Yeah, thanks for rubbing that in. Appreciate it."

Jas slung an arm across his shoulders. "We're only teasing because we care about you so much."

Teagan's boyfriend Lucas leaned forward. He'd said little throughout the conversation, probably because this was personal stuff and he didn't know them that well. "Just ask her out. She can only say no."

"Even then it won't be the end of the world," said Teagan. "I knocked Lucas back a heap of times before I went anywhere with him."

Lucas reached across to squeeze Teagan's fingers. "Wore her down in the end."

"Em and I had our moments too," said Josh, serious now. "And look where we are."

Jas gave Harry another friendly squeeze and a peck on the cheek. "Cheer up, big boy. You have us on your side now. And thanks to Em booking Summer to do our makeup, we'll have her all to ourselves. Hours in which to sing your praises. She won't stand a chance."

A statement that offered Harry no comfort at all.

***

Summer smiled at Jasmine Thomas and indicated the chair she'd readied in the living room of Emily Wallace-Jones's gorgeous limestone and dolomite house at Rocking Horse Hill. Summer's makeup kit, which looked more like a handyman's toolbox, was open on the small table she'd placed nearby. Grace was busy with Emily, her product and tool trays arranged on an exquisitely finished art desk – a present, Summer had learned, from Emily's furniture craftsman fiancé Josh.

Mother of the bride, Adrienne Wallace-Jones, was hovering in the kitchen with Emily's grandmother, arguing over the optimum time to thin a fig crop for the best sized early fruit. Jasmine and Teagan were gossiping about some mutual friends, while Emily was telling Grace about the property's historic Avenue of Honour and the fallen soldiers the trees represented. No one seemed to be interested in discussing the approaching wedding at all.

The view from the enormous windows of Emily's lounge was spectacular. The magnificent slopes of Rocking Horse Hill, the district's famous volcanic cone and crater, rose up before them in ever-changing colour. The day was fine with only a few high white clouds dotting the sky, a relief for all who knew how fickle the local weather could be, even in early November.

The windows filled the room with light and made working conditions perfect. Adrienne had laid out plates of tiny fruit friands, mini cupcakes and other delights, and the kitchen was redolent with the scent of good coffee. With the exception of Teagan who was drinking mineral water, the ladies had started preparations with a celebratory flute of French champagne. Summer had refused the offer of a glass. She was attending both bridesmaids and wanted to keep a steady hand. Plus she felt it was somewhat unprofessional. Grace, she noticed, had no such qualms. Her boss, to Summer's bemusement, seemed to be acting as though she was part of the Wallace-Jones fold instead of a contractor. Although to Summer's eye, Grace's attempts at chumminess appeared to be tolerated rather than appreciated.

Jasmine settled down, eyeing Summer a little too intently. From the moment Summer was introduced, she'd noticed that all three girls had shown undue interest in her. They'd been nice, very nice in fact, but Summer couldn't help feeling unnerved at their attention. She hoped it wasn't anything to do with Harry. He might not have complained to Grace about her, but he could have mentioned something to Emily, Jasmine or Teagan. Although why Emily would then specifically request her for today was baffling.

"I hear you're a horse girl," said Jasmine.

"Yes. I have a dressage horse. I used to do eventing but with working full time it's too hard to keep him fit enough."

"You're from the upper south-east, is that right?" This was Teagan, who'd swapped water for a cup of coffee and was propped on the arm of a sofa.

Summer nodded. "From Haikenvale, near Keith. I moved down here a couple of months ago."

"Levenham's a lovely town," said Adrienne, leaving the kitchen to sit near her daughter.

"No thanks to that idiot Councillor Herriott," added Emily's very grand grandmother, wandering over in a waft of lingering cigar smoke and expensive perfume. Summer was secretly glad it would be Grace tackling the elderly lady's makeup. With her clipped voice, beautifully cut clothes and sharp gaze, Granny B, as she insisted on being called, was an intimidating woman. Even more so given she was on her second glass of champagne and showing no hint of stopping. "But what can one expect from a vegetarian. Ridiculous people." She slipped a look at Summer. "I do hope you're not one. Can't have you attaching yourself to –"

"Gran!"

Granny B sniffed, then twitched a smile at Summer. Without another word she strode off, releasing a short sharp whistle as she walked. Emily's dog, who'd been dozing in a patch of sunshine near the kitchen's sliding glass door, shot to attention. "Come along, Miss Muffet." And with that she popped an unlit cigar between her teeth and stomped out.

"Sorry about that," said Emily. "Gran has a thing about vegetarians."

"Just as well I like a good steak then."

Jasmine, Teagan and Emily all exchanged a weirdly pleased glance that made Summer fumble with her makeup brush. Like three perched owls they stared back at her, sharing identical wide-eyed smiles. If Grace wasn't in the room, Summer would have downed tools and asked them what was up, but she wasn't about to do that while her boss was around.

Summer carried on, silently lamenting her refusal of champagne. Alcohol might have helped settle her nerves. Which was ironic, considering her clients were the ones who were meant to be nervous, but this was the most unruffled bridal party she'd ever encountered.

Doing her best to ignore their odd behaviour, she settled into work, smoothing on foundation and dabbing concealer, using her brushes to highlight and shade, playing down faults and emphasising assets. Losing herself in technique and artistry.

"You keep your horse at Gavin Chalk's?" asked Emily.

"Oh, do you?" said Adrienne. "I heard he had a terrible turn. I don't suppose you know if he's home from hospital yet?"

"Not yet. But it should be soon." Although the awful way Gav had lain pasty, trembling and defeated in his hospital bed, barely able to maintain eye contact when she visited him earlier that morning, Summer wished they'd keep him in.

"He was a lovely man before alcohol took him" said Adrienne. "It was so sad the way he fell apart when his wife died. A few of us tried to help, but he shut himself away and rejected all our efforts."

"They never had children, did they?" asked Emily.

"No," replied her mother "I have a feeling Barbara couldn't. Although they always seemed happy enough, which is no doubt why he was so devastated when she died. All they had was each other."

"Poor Gav," said Summer, staring momentarily into

space. His loneliness must be incredibly painful. She could almost understand the need to numb it.

Adrienne toyed with an amber-and-gold earring, her brow slightly crinkled. "We should arrange some help for when he comes home."

"I've been trying," said Summer. "Taking him meals and helping him as much as I can, but it's his drinking that's the real problem."

"Yes, and not an easy one to conquer." Adrienne considered further. "Leave it with me. I'll talk to Samuel – he's my partner – and see what we can arrange."

"Thanks." Eyes down, she fiddled with the eyeliner pencil she'd been using. "I worry about him."

"It's kind of you to do so, Summer. Not many would bother."

When Summer looked up she found not three people regarding her with that weird wide-eyed look again, but four. Grace, whose gaze was sullen and narrowed, was the only odd one out.

Not liking her boss's expression, Summer hastily returned to work, wondering when the wedding excitement was going to kick in. Not any time soon if the way the women were acting was a guide. This would have to be the most chilled-out wedding party she'd encountered, and that included the group who'd decided on a Rocky Horror Picture Show theme, complete with Frank N. Furter groom and Janet bride in a pointy bra and high-waisted knickers. Although Summer suspected that group's laid back attitude had more to do with a certain herbal helper than natural nonchalance.

To Summer's relief, the conversation switched to local news and events, spiced by the return of Granny B, who seemed to know everything and everyone and had an opinion on all. It was only when Jasmine's makeup was finished and Teagan took her seat that Summer realised her respite was over.

"We really enjoyed our spa sessions on Saturday, didn't we?" Teagan remarked.

Jasmine and Emily nodded.

"The boys did too," said Emily.

"Some more than others," murmured Jasmine, causing Summer to look up sharply, but Jasmine's expression was pure innocence.

"I told you they would," said Adrienne. "I bet they all sneak back for another round."

"Harry definitely plans to," said Teagan.

"Rather eligible young man, our Harry." Granny B cast a pointed look at Summer. "Solid family, the Argyles. Excellent property. Good-looking fellow, too. Tall and broad of shoulder. Rather large feet and hands." She nodded knowingly. "You know what they say about those."

"Gran."

"What?" Granny B blinked at her granddaughter.

"Just don't."

"Never mind Granny B," said Jasmine to Summer. "She's only miffed that Harry knocked her back."

"Oh, Mum," said Adrienne, "you didn't."

Granny B hoisted her chin. "I'm an eighty-year-old woman in fine fettle. I can, and will, proposition whomever I like." She slid a look and wink toward the bridesmaids. "One even scores a yes every now and then."

Teagan and Jasmine clapped and hooted with laughter.

Emily covered her ears and shook her head but there was no hiding the smile on her face. Cheeks pinking, Adrienne huffed and threw appalled glances at her mother. Summer could only grin at the old lady who winked back. She was proving a naughty woman, that Granny B. Formidable, certainly, but fun.

When they'd all settled down, the girls resumed their wide-eyed owl routine.

"So," said Teagan, "how did you find Harry?"

She flicked a peek at Grace who, from the way her mouth was puckered, was clearly feeling put out by their interest in Summer. "He was a very good client."

"Harry mentioned that he was there when you found Gavin," said Emily.

"Not quite. I'd already called the ambulance when he turned up. It was a comfort to have him there though. He seemed to know what he was doing more than me."

"That'd be his training," said Jasmine. "He's been a State Emergency Service volunteer for years. He stayed to help you afterwards?"

"Yes." Summer was grateful for it too. Gav's mess was enough to turn her own stomach, but Harry had simply got on with it and hadn't complained once.

"He's like that. Always ready to lend a hand."

Granny B wandered back from the kitchen. "We appear to have run out of champagne."

"That's because I only bought two bottles, Gran."

"Only two? Really, Emily, I thought we brought you up better than that." Granny B turned her blue eyes on Summer. "He's single, you know."

Emily released what sounded like an extremely frustrated sigh and shook her head.

"Your own fault," said Jasmine, patting her friend's shoulder. "You're the one who told her."

"I know, I know."

"Sorry," murmured Teagan as Summer bent close to feather some bronze shadow around the corner of Teagan's eye. "Subtlety never has been Granny B's forte."

"I heard that, young Teagan."

Teagan grinned. Grace slapped down a brush with undue force.

Finally clocking where their odd behaviour was stemming from, Summer swallowed. "Oh." She added a non-committal smile for good measure, and tried to concentrate on her task, but her cheeks were on fire and her clients were back gawking at her.

Summer's mind continued to spin. Had Harry put them up to this? Surely not. He'd be far too embarrassed and she couldn't imagine him telling anyone about what happened during the massage. Now that she considered it, he had acted odd during their last meeting. Too worried for Gav and desperate to get to the hospital, she hadn't given it much thought at the time. Looking back though, he'd been all action man during the crisis, before settling into helpfulness. But when it had come time to leave, it was if he hadn't wanted to. He'd even asked if she wanted him to accompany her to the hospital. Summer had dismissed it as typical country kindness, the sort of thing anyone would do, but perhaps there was more to it.

The urge to probe was enormous but she wasn't about to do anything of the sort while Grace was eavesdropping. And in a temper.

Unfortunately, none of the others felt inclined to let it go.

"Harry's a good bloke," said Teagan.

"If you don't count his gormlessness around women," said Jasmine.

"Jas." Emily shot her friend a frown.

"Come on, you have to admit he can be a bit clumsy. Remember his efforts with Maya?" She addressed Summer. "Maya Higgins is the girl Harry's had a crush on forever. At least he did until you came along. Every time he tried to ask her out he'd get all bumbly and stuttery, which made her think he was a complete dill, when he's not. Not really. It's just that he spends so much time fretting about saying the right thing he either says nothing or can't get the words out properly."

"Digby used to be like that," said Adrienne sadly. "Before . . ." She waved a hand toward the window and Rocking Horse Hill.

"Not a subject for today," snapped Granny B. Then she smiled and stroked Emily's hair, her tone softening. "Today is for celebrations. Even if we are rather lacking in champagne to do it with."

"It's not even eleven, Gran. We still have to have our hair done yet. Any more and you'll be snoring in church."

"I should think not. Unlike some, I can hold my drink."

"I thought we were meant to be setting up Harry?" remarked Jasmine.

Except for Adrienne, who remained staring at the hill, they all focused back on Summer; Jasmine with her eyebrow raised, Emily and Granny B with expectant expressions, Teagan with a sympathetic smile, and Grace with a vinegary look of disapproval.

The only way to fob them off was with the reminder

of what they were all here for: wedding preparations. "You're not helping me keep a steady hand here, you know."

A series of muttered sorrys followed, although only Emily's sounded sincere.

"You're staying on for the church photos, aren't you?" asked Jasmine. "In case we all bawl and ruin our faces?"

"I –"

"I'll take care of that," said Grace.

"That won't be necessary," said Granny B, dismissing Grace in a tone that sounded more posh and regal than ever. She smiled but it contained more steel than humour. We wouldn't want to keep you from the spa. You are the manager, after all. Summer will be fine."

Grace opened her mouth to object but Granny B continued in that clipped, entitled voice that demanded she have her way. "The girls want her. This is their day."

Grace's expression was as sweetly brittle as thin toffee. "Of course."

"Excellent." Granny B clapped her hands, happy she had her way. "That settles it then."

Teagan patted Summer's arm. "They're only doing it because they love Harry so much."

"And we like you," said Jasmine.

Summer regarded them with dismay. "But you don't even know me."

"You're a horse girl," said Teagan.

"And Harry has a crush on you," added Jasmine.

"And you're not vegetarian." Granny B gave a theatrical shudder and then stopped to peer at her. "Although you aren't one of those teetotallers, are you? That would be quite unacceptable."

"Oi," said Teagan.

Granny B gave a dismissive wave. "You don't count."

"I don't mind a glass of wine," Summer admitted.

"Well then," said Granny B.

Emily spread her hands, eyes alight with merriment. "Nothing much more to know."

Summer felt a strange compulsion to giggle at the surrealness of it all. Instead she picked up a narrow makeup brush, dusted it with shadow, and went to work on Teagan's eyelids, trying not to think about big Harry.

And failing dismally.

FIVE

Harry was hot. The hired, three-piece wedding suit he was wearing may as well have been made of rubber. The church's stained glass windows, so admired, were concentrating shafts of stifling sunlight right onto the altar area, and to make life even more unpleasant he was suffering a vicious attack of nerves.

His stomach felt strung tighter than a new fence and his palms remained greasy, no matter how often Harry surreptitiously wiped them with the emergency hanky his mum had forced into his pocket. Thank God. Harry hoped like hell the deodorant he'd applied only a few hours before lived up to its "fresh for 48 hours" claim. At the rate he was metabolising, it was like cramming a week's worth of living into a day. Even the soothing sound of the church organ didn't calm him. If anything, it made him worse.

What was more annoying was that his state had nothing to do with what was about to take place. Harry had no problems with the wedding. After all, it wasn't him about to get hitched. All Harry had to do was hang around looking supportive, then lead Teagan back out of the church, making sure she didn't trip over. Dead easy.

Facing Summer at the end of it, however, was not.

She'd spent half a day with a bunch of overexcited

women who were hell-bent on managing his love life. The thought of what they could have told her, the secrets that could have been revealed, their ruminations on his character and attributes, was horrifying. What if Jas had explained to Summer what a tool he was? Or how they were being kind and "helping" him because Harry was too useless to help himself? She'd think he was a complete dick.

"You right there, big fella?"

"Yep." Harry twitched a smile at Josh who, to his irritation, was displaying no sign of nerves at all.

The only indications of Josh's state of mind were the glances he kept throwing toward the end of the church and the anticipation brightening his eyes. Not a forehead shine or fidgeting hand to be seen. Harry shouldn't have been surprised. Josh was like that before footy too, all calm focus, while Harry would be quivering like a racehorse in the barriers.

It was enough to make a bloke feel jealous. Which he was. Not for Josh's coolness — he was used to that — but of the life Josh was about to embark on. Although truth was, Josh had been enjoying his new life with Em for a while now, after moving from his parents' house out to Rocking Horse Hill. But marriage somehow made it different, gave it permanence, and acted as a symbol of all Josh felt for Em. What they felt for each other. No doubt there'd be kids in the near future too. More milestones to celebrate.

What did Harry have? A thriving property that kept him and his brother Eddie busy. A farmhouse that used to belong to his grandparents that he called home. Good friends, family, sport. A well-trained dog. Not a bad life, when you added it all up. Except it was missing that thing that made the world special and filled a man's existence with true meaning.

He'd hoped Maya would be that thing. And he'd tried, but you couldn't make someone love you, and she sure as fuck didn't. But Summer . . .

For all he knew any chance with her was now ruined thanks to a bunch of gossipy girls and his own big mouth. The thought had Harry sneaking his hands again into his trouser pockets to rub his palms dry.

A few coughs sounded from the pews. One of the ushers signalled. The moment had come.

First to appear were Josh's parents and grandparents, their faces split with proud smiles. They made their way down the aisle, pausing for a moment near the altar to speak quickly to Josh before taking their seats on the right hand side of the church. Granny B and Em's mum, Adrienne, appeared next at the door where they waited for the Sinclairs to be seated and the usher to return.

Granny B, resplendent in a form-fitting sea-green dress and cropped jacket, and sporting a monster-sized hat decorated with feathers and stiff bows, grinned and waved at Josh and Digby before throwing Harry a cheeky wink. Adrienne, equally stunning in burgundy but with a less ostentatious hat, was already delicately dabbing at tears.

"Showtime," Josh murmured, as the families settled into the front pews. Though he straightened his suit and attempted to look serious, nothing could keep the pure joy Josh was feeling from breaking through.

Reverend Ellis, who'd been chatting quietly to Digby, motioned them to take position. All that was required now was the bride.

"Good luck, mate," said Harry, shaking Josh's hand. He settled next to Digby and cast him a glance, only to start at the sight of him. The best man was pale and swallowing heavily, as if any moment he'd collapse in a faint.

Harry went into immediate action. He stepped in front of Digby, using his broad back and height to protect the man from view. "You right there, Dig?" he asked, keeping his voice low.

"Yeah." Digby blinked several times. "Yes, I'm right."

Poor bastard. Harry couldn't imagine what Digby was feeling right now. Loss, he guessed. Grief. Maybe even bitterness. Here his sister was, about to get married in the church where only a year ago Digby had been planning to do the same with his fiancée, Felicity. The man had to be hurting.

"Dig?" Josh had also turned and was staring with worry.

"I'm right." Except he didn't sound or look it.

Harry met Josh's eyes, and curled his hand over Digby's shoulder. "If you can't handle this, you'd better say so now."

Digby swallowed some more, his breath shaky. He was blinking rapidly, droplets of moisture clinging to his eyelashes. He took two more long breaths. "I can handle it."

"You sure?"

"Yes." Harry watched in relief as some of Digby's stoicism returned and he regarded Josh. "I won't let you down. Not after what you did for me." He swallowed again. "And her."

Josh indulged in a brief man-hug, a sign of the bond they'd formed, a bond that went beyond being future brothers-in-law. Josh let go and glanced at the Reverend, who was observing them with concern. "We're good."

Reverend Ellis nodded, but his gaze was on Digby.

"Jas'll be here in a tick," said Harry, but the comment didn't seem to provide Digby with any comfort. If anything it made his face set, leaving Harry to wonder if perhaps he and Teagan were wrong about those two. Maybe they were just having no-strings sex. People did stuff like that. Not him – that wasn't Harry's way – but he knew of plenty who did.

At least the drama had one benefit: it took Harry's mind off Summer and served as a reminder that there were others in the world who had more worries and regrets than him.

Reverend Ellis stepped close to murmur something to Digby, who replied equally quietly. Satisfied, the Reverend smiled at Josh and all three of them turned again to face the aisle. Harry caught Granny B's eye and gave her a sneaky thumbs up. The old lady's puckered mouth relaxed in relief. She turned to Adrienne and spoke for a few seconds, then leaned across to address Adrienne's partner, Samuel. After a bit of shuffling and whispers, the trio seemed to settle, although Adrienne never let her gaze stray far from her anguished son.

A hush fell. Like a mob of meerkats, the congregation all turned their faces and strained toward the door. A hundred cameras were lifted in expectation. There was a brief pause and then the organist began belting out the wedding march.

Teagan stepped forward, looking gorgeous in a dark

blue strapless silky dress and holding a white bouquet. Jas followed, her eyes suspiciously shiny. Flashes went off, filling the church with even more light. The flower girl and page boy stumbled forward, holding hands and looking awed. A chorus of "Ahs" were breathed at their cuteness.

Finally came Em, her hand tucked in the crook of her father's arm. Her posture was confident, her step dignified. Like her husband-to-be, not a trace of anxiety affected her, only happiness. She smiled graciously, nodding at people as she passed but always returning her eyes forward, to where Josh stood with a stupid, almost disbelieving grin on his face.

Harry couldn't blame him. Em was strikingly, breath-snatchingly beautiful, like a princess or a movie star. She'd always been attractive, but today had transformed her into someone else.

Her gown sat just off her shoulders, and folded across her chest in a series of pleats before nipping into her slim waist and blooming outward in a plain, floor-length sheath. The design was elegant, simple, and very Em. Unlike the plain white bouquets the bridesmaids carried, Em's flowers were mixed with a smaller blue bloom. Her only jewellery appeared to be a pair of sparkling diamond and sapphire earrings.

For a moment, Harry's eyesight went a bit hazy with soppy sentimentality. Then he remembered the import of the moment and that he still had a whole ceremony to get through. Not to mention a rocky best man to support.

"You look beautiful," he said to Teagan as Em was delivered to Josh and they took their places.

"Thanks." She gave him a light nudge. "You haven't

scrubbed up too badly either." Her humour disappeared as she focused on the best man. "Is Digby all right?"

"Yeah. He's just a bit, you know."

Her expression saddened. "Yes. God knows, Felicity had her faults but Digby thought the world of her. All he wanted was to marry, start a family. Make them both complete. This has to be tough for him."

Jas was doing her best to keep Digby together. Her fingers were tangled with his and she was talking softly, but whatever had afflicted Digby earlier was fading. Colour had returned to his face and he appeared to be breathing normally again, giving Harry confidence he'd endure. Besides, Digby had promised, and while his feelings toward his sister were mixed, Harry had every faith Digby wouldn't let Josh down.

The bride and groom were staring at one another with secretive smiles, as if only they knew how special this moment was, and once again Harry was overcome with sentimentality. Unable to help himself, he shot a quick, hopeful look toward the back of the church.

And damn near squeaked.

Summer was hovering at the very rear, looking heart-stoppingly sweet and pretty in a flowery knee-length dress and her hair tied up in a loose bun. She was standing with her hands folded in front of the skirt, a silver toolbox by her feet, and gazing at one of the church's colourful stained glass windows. As he gawked, the window was hit by a shaft of sunlight, dappling her face and body in colour. And though Harry knew it probably ranked as one of the dumbest notions he'd ever been struck with, he couldn't help feeling as though, somehow, the building was blessing her.

He continued to gawp, willing her to look at him, if only for a second, but Teagan tugged on his sleeve. "Eyes forward. We're on."

Right. The wedding.

Harry quickly refocused, taking special care to keep his back straight and head up. Knowing Summer was watching should have resurrected his nerves but seeing her there, bathed in church light, had filled him with renewed hope.

Maybe one day this would be him too.

***

"I must say, young Harry," said Granny B, waving her tumbler of Scotch his way, "you're looking rather dishy in that suit."

Used to her now, Harry bent and kissed her heavily powdered cheek. "You're looking pretty fit yourself, Granny B."

"Thank you. I must admit to feeling it too, although weddings do tend to bring out the best in one." She nodded toward Digby. "Bit touch and go there for a while, wasn't it?"

"A bit."

She studied Digby a little longer. "He and Jasmine are sleeping together, although attempting to hide the fact. Not doing a very good job. It's the small things that give it away. Touches when they think no one is watching. The meeting of eyes that last a little too long." She grimaced. "That's the problem with getting old. Too much wisdom too late." Raising her tumbler, Granny B took a hearty slug. "I'm not convinced it will last, but we shall see. Even if it is temporary it's certainly a relief from where he seemed headed." She refocused on Harry. "Speaking of heading places, we had a good chat with your beautician this morning."

Harry took a hasty swig of beer. Granny B was in on it too? This was not good news. Not good news at all. "Oh, yeah?"

"She's from Haikenvale, you know."

No, Harry didn't. He hardly knew anything about Summer except that she was pretty, liked horses, and made him feel soppy and protective and bursting with pathetic longing. He wondered what had brought her to Levenham. People his age on the move tended to choose Adelaide over the regional towns, for the greater job prospects and exciting lifestyle. Not that Harry would know. He'd never lived anywhere other than here.

"Seems a nice girl. Not vegetarian either." Granny B pressed the tumbler against Harry's arm and nodded sagely. "Although do make sure you do your homework. If only for your mother's sake."

He took a moment to study her. Harry might be a bit slow sometimes but Granny B was no one's fool. "Do you know something about her? Something bad?"

"No." She threaded another look through the gathering toward her grandson. "But none of us want another Digby on our hands. We've all suffered enough pain from that." And with that comment, she strode off.

With Digby steadfast in his refusal to ever step another foot on Rocking Horse Hill, but with the crater and property holding great meaning for Em and Josh, the wedding couple had been forced to make compromises. The majority of the wedding photos had been taken at various locations around Levenham, ending here at Camrick, the Wallace-Jones's historic mansion near the centre of town. Em and Josh had then dumped everyone under the backyard marquee to kick back with pre-reception drinks and nibbles, and headed to Rocking Horse Hill for a series of final shots, taking Summer with them.

Although she'd been present for the entire shoot, dashing powder onto shiny faces, fixing mascara stains and topping up lipstick, other than exchanging shy smiles, Harry had had no opportunity to talk to her. He'd assumed she'd head off the moment the photos were complete but Em had whispered that neither of them would escape so easily, and promised she'd invite Summer back to join them.

The idea, according to the girls, who had it all gleefully planned out, was for Harry to take his chance and talk to her. Not for long, because they had a reception to attend, but enough to charm Summer and ask her out for dinner, his idea of drinks having been vetoed on the grounds that it was far too unromantic. Now, with the sick feeling Granny B had left him churning over, he didn't know if he could do it. What if she wasn't who he hoped she was? What if she had horrible secrets, or had been in jail, or was an ex-bikie chick, or had an abandoned husband and five kids hidden somewhere?

Worst of all, what if she was just like Maya and thought he was a complete dick not worthy of her interest?

Harry swallowed another mouthful of beer and tried not to panic.

Everyone turned at the sound of a car in the drive.

Harry faced the marquee's open flap, his heart thudding as he waited for the bride and groom and, hopefully, Summer to appear. The minutes ticked like hours. Finally a cheer went up at Em's and Josh's arrival, followed by a rush of people crowding around, offering drinks, back slaps and hugs. The photographer stepped through, tripod under one arm, case slung over the other shoulder, and wound his way carefully toward Adrienne. Harry kept his focus, his fingers tight around his stubbie holder.

Seconds passed. Long, desperate ones.

Harry hovered, uncertain. He glanced toward Em and Josh but they were busy with well-wishers who wouldn't be attending the reception, but had dropped by to see the bride and groom and share a celebratory drink. He hunted for Teagan but she was occupied with Lucas. Jasmine was head to head with Digby, her hand stroking the small of his back. Harry searched for Granny B but she'd collared the mayor and Samuel, and was engaged in what appeared to be a very hearty discussion. No one was paying him the slightest attention, most likely because they were too embarrassed.

His head dropped. She wasn't coming. Which could only mean one thing.

Harry sighed and rubbed his head, and cast one more look through the open flap.

And locked gazes with Summer.

A grin leaped across his face, then wobbled as her expression remained neutral. Summer's gaze flicked around the marquee and back to him. She rubbed her forearm and shifted a little, then the corner of her mouth lifted in a shy smile that had Harry's chest ballooning with relief.

He crossed over to her. "Hi."

"Hi."

He swung his arm toward the bar. "Can I get you a drink? There's champagne." At her hesitation he went on. "Or there's wine, and beer. Soft drink, too. There might even be some spirits. Definitely Scotch. Whatever you want. I think there's tea and coffee somewhere. Water." He frowned. "Probably fruit juice." Realising he was gabbling, he winced and stared somewhere above her head.

"A glass of champagne would be nice."

"Okay. Good. Good. I'll, ah, go get it then." He nodded. "You'll stay here?"

She rubbed her arm again. "Sure."

"Good. That's great. Really great. I'll be right back. Don't move." Before he could make an even bigger fool of himself, Harry quickly turned and hurried toward the bar.

"Idiot," he muttered, as he waited. "Moron. Dickhead."

"That's the way to psyche yourself," said Josh, grinning as he joined Harry. "Self abuse. Works every time."

"Don't you start." He nodded to the barman. "Beer and a champagne, thanks." He turned back to Josh. "How's it feel?"

Immediately, Josh's gaze drifted to his wife. "Magic."

"Rub it in, why don't you?"

"It's my wedding day. I'm allowed." Josh picked up his beer, clinked it against Harry's and nodded toward Summer. "Good luck."

"Thanks." The way Harry was faring, he'd bloody

need it.

The shy smile she'd blessed him with earlier had vanished. Summer seemed hesitant again, gnawing on her lip and rubbing her arm as she stared around, as if worried she was intruding. Harry supposed he couldn't blame her. The only reason she was here was because of the machinations of the girls, all of whom were slyly watching right now.

He held the champagne flute out to her.

"Thanks." She took a sip. "Well, this is embarrassing."

"Why? You don't like it? I'll go change it. There's plenty of other stuff to drink."

She giggled a little. "No. The champagne's fine." She tilted her head and lifted her eyebrows. "I meant, everyone watching us."

Harry checked. The wedding party had ceased trying to be sly and were openly gawking. He resisted the urge to give them all the finger, and tried to concentrate on Summer and the fact she was here, talking to him, as though she wanted to.

"Oh. Sorry about them," he said.

"I guess they worry about you."

"Just a bit." He didn't want to talk about the others and he sure as hell could do without them all goggling like that. In an effort to foil their efforts, he stepped around so his back was to them. "So did it, ah, go well?"

Is that what you asked beauticians? Harry had no idea. Maybe he should have asked about Binky.

"It was fine. Emily's so lovely she hardly needs makeup. We climbed Rocking Horse Hill. The view was amazing."

"Yeah, it is. Been a while since I was up there though.

How's Binky?"

"He's good," she replied slowly, throwing him a look he couldn't interpret.

Harry nodded and rubbed the back of his neck. "And, ah, Gav?"

"He's not so good."

"Oh. Sorry." Realising he'd fucked up, Harry swallowed and tried to think of a new subject but he was at a loss.

Summer took a tiny sip of champagne and balanced the flute base on her palm. She surveyed the guests, scraping the corner of her bottom lip with her front teeth. The silence between them dragged on, becoming more and more awkward with each heartbeat. Harry opened his mouth, shut it, and stared at the open marquee flap in dismay.

Summer followed his gaze and frowned. For a moment she remained silent, contemplating her wine glass, then she indicated the exit. "I guess . . ."

"You're leaving?"

"I probably should." She checked the silver watch circling her wrist. "Binky's probably planning his escape as we speak. Hunger tends to make him cunning."

"Right. Okay. Sure." Harry puffed out a breath and scratched the back of his neck again. "I'll walk you to your car."

"You don't have to. I'm fine."

"I want to."

"Okay." And this time when she smiled, it contained no hesitation. Only delight.

Harry took her glass and placed it and his beer on a table, deliberately avoiding any eye contact with his friends, and returned to Summer's side. As she moved off, he went to place his palm onto the curve of her back above her waist, and let it hover. Was that the right thing to do? Maybe not. Some women got all funny about being touched. Then again, during his massage she'd had her hands all over him. A semi-naked him as well. And with a hard-on.

Harry decided to risk it, but moved his hand further toward the middle and kept it feather-light. At his touch, Summer glanced his way and smiled, causing Harry to grin with relief in return. Perhaps it would be all right after all.

The chattery marquee noise faded as they crunched along the length of Camrick's gravel drive, dodging rows of cars. The street was full too. One part of Harry hoped Summer hadn't been forced to park too far away, while the other wished it was miles. Anything to extend his time with her.

"I'm just down there." She pointed past a red hatchback to where her silver SUV was parked.

Bugger. Too close. And he still hadn't thought of anything clever to say.

Summer solved the problem for him. "You look different all done up."

"Different?" Was that good? Christ, he hoped so.

"Quite sophisticated."

Heat flared across Harry's cheeks. Sophisticated was definitely good. It had a James Bond kind of ring.

"Thanks." He took a couple more steps. "I saw you in the church. You were looking at one of the windows. I thought . . ." He breathed out and halted.

Summer turned, head tilted. The sun was falling now.

Its peach glow tickled her shoulders and hair, making her even prettier than when he'd seen her standing under the light of the stained glass window. And Harry once again had the overwhelming feeling that she was being blessed. That this was right. That she was right. If only he could find the gumption to seize the moment.

One breath, two breaths. Summer's bemused expression began to falter.

Harry's words came out in a torrent. "I thought you looked really pretty. Look, are we okay? Cos I've been nothing but a dick, what with yelling at you and getting a hard-on and everything, and my friends telling you God knows what. But I'm not . . . a dick, that is. Well, I try not to be. I just get . . ."

"Tongue-tied. I heard."

"Yeah."

They shared a smile.

"We're okay, Harry."

"We are?"

"Yes, we are."

Harry was about to float off into the sky, he felt so light-headed with relief and hope. "Okay enough for me to ask you out to dinner?"

"Sure. Why not?"

Harry wanted to whoop. Actually, that was a lie. What he really wanted to do was kiss her. Instead he did neither of those things. He stood in the middle of the footpath like the idiot he was and simply grinned.

"Harry?"

"Yeah?"

"You mentioned dinner?"

"Oh, yeah. Right. Is tomorrow night too soon?"

She laughed. "Just a little. Why don't you call me when you've worked it out?"

"Okay, whatever you want. Hang on, I don't have your number."

Summer solved the problem by opening the boot of her wagon and digging around in the makeup kit she'd stowed there. She waved one of the spa's business cards at him before scribbling down her number using an eyebrow pencil.

"There," she said, holding it out to him.

"Thanks."

"I'd better get going." She nodded toward Camrick. "And you'd better get back."

He nodded, pocketing the card and opening the front door for her, then closing it as she settled inside.

She started the engine and wound down the window. "Enjoy your night."

"I will." Stealing a few seconds more, he leaned close to the window. "Say g'day to Binky for me."

"I will." Her smile was as pinkly luscious as one of his mum's perfect rose buds. Checking the front of her car against the rear of one ahead, she dropped a hand to the gear shift. Harry couldn't help it, he leaned through the open window to kiss her cheek, except she'd been about to turn back to him and the kiss landed right on her mouth.

Startled, they both pulled away but a half-breath later Harry's palm was cupping her smooth neck and his eyes were closing and his mouth was back on hers. Not for long. The kiss was brief, not much more than a connection of mouths, but that didn't prevent it from being the softest, most heart-stopping kiss he'd ever experienced.

Backing out fast, he retreated to the footpath before he did anything else stupid.

"I'll call," he promised.

"Okay."

To Harry her voice sounded husky. With want? Shock? He wanted to ask but couldn't. At least she hadn't pushed him away. If anything, she'd responded.

With a last, encouraging smile, Summer put the car into gear and reversed to give herself space to pull out. Satisfied she had clearance, she switched to first, and after checking mirrors drove forward, only to suddenly brake and lean her head out the window.

"Harry?"

"What?"

Summer grinned in a way that shot his heart into orbit. "Call soon."

SIX

Summer closed her hand over Gav's big fist. "It'll be all right."

They were seated at the kitchen table, empty tea mugs in front of them. The back door was open to let in the mild evening air but the house retained a faint odour of bleach from Summer's scrubbing. She'd worked all Sunday morning on it, not wanting Gav to arrive home only to be slapped in the face with reminders of his bender. The man was fragile enough, in need of a sanctuary of peace and comfort instead of distress. But so far he'd made no comment. She wasn't even sure he'd noticed.

A community nurse had ferried him from the hospital and settled him in. Summer didn't know if he'd talked much to her, but he certainly wasn't talking to Summer, and eye contact appeared out of the question.

She didn't know what else to say. She needed to get home, have some dinner and an early night, but the way Gav was acting she was scared to leave him on his own.

"Do you want me to stay with you?"

He shook his head. "You've done enough."

Summer squeezed his fingers. "I don't mind."

"I'll be all right."

"Gav —"

"I said I'll be all right!"

Summer sucked in her lips and stared into the bottom of her cup. Then she sighed quietly, pushed her chair back and stood. "I'll see you tomorrow after work." She willed Gav to look at her but his head remained turned away. A slight tremble affected his sagging jowls and his fisted fingers were twitching. She blinked as approaching tears of sympathy began to sting her eyes. "Please, if you need anything, call me. It doesn't matter what time. I'll come."

Summer was at the door when he finally spoke. His voice was croaky, as though scraped from his lungs. "Why?"

Why indeed? Guilt, for one. Compassion and kindness another. How could anyone stand by and let this essentially decent man self-destruct? Not her.

"My grandpa was just like you. Watching one person kill themselves with drink is enough for one lifetime. I don't want another."

Gav's gaze dropped to the table surface and stayed there. Summer tapped the door frame and waited a few seconds longer. When he remained silent, she headed out into the dark. Having finished his dinner, Binky was by the side fence, waiting for her. His soft brown eyes reminded her of Harry's and she wished it was him standing there instead of her horse, arms open in readiness to fold her protectively against his solid, steadfast chest. But Harry was on his farm, and Binky would have to do. She took a moment to press her face into his neck and take comfort in his reliable bulk.

She released a long sigh, wishing she had someone to pass this burden on to. Gav wasn't her grandfather. He wasn't even her responsibility. His life was his own to destroy. Except she could no more not care about Gav than any other creature. If a dog or horse or any other animal were hurting she'd do something to help. It was how she'd been brought up, part of her belief system. The question was, in this case, what to do?

A dilemma Summer spent the evening mulling over. Between eyeing her phone wondering when Harry would call, that is. By the end of the night when she tucked into bed, Summer had no answer and, even more disappointingly, no dinner date.

So much for Harry's enthusiasm.

At ten on Monday morning, not long after the spa had opened, Granny B sailed regally into reception, unapologetically interrupting Grace in the middle of her weekly staff pep talk, and commandeered Summer. Taking her by the elbow, Granny B steered Summer aside, calling over her shoulder to Grace that she was just borrowing her employee for a few minutes and to please carry on.

If she weren't so scared of reprisals, Summer would have broken into giggles.

"Bit of a sourpuss your boss, isn't she?" said Granny B, having escorted Summer out onto the street and into a delicious patch of morning sunshine.

"She's all right."

Granny B gave her an approving look. "Good girl. Never pays to bad-mouth one's boss. You never know who might be listening." She bent close, one heavily plucked and pencilled eyebrow raised. "You do realise her father was once a garbage collector?" Granny B nodded. "Remember that next time she tries to look down her nose at you."

"I'll try."

"Good. Now, did you enjoy yourself on Saturday?"

"I did. The wedding was beautiful." Summer thought she knew what Granny B was up to, and braced herself for questions about Harry, but the old lady surprised her.

"It was, indeed. Emily made a stunning bride. Rather like myself. It's our excellent Wallace genes." She patted Summer's hand. "Now tell me, how is our Gavin coping at home?"

"I don't know. He's not saying much and he could barely look at me yesterday." Summer tried to keep the anguish out of her voice, but she'd had a horrible night's sleep thanks to her worry over Gav, and was feeling tired and upset. Plus Harry hadn't called. "I just wish I knew how to help."

"Dealing with alcoholics is never easy."

"I know. My grandfather was one."

"Yes, so I discovered." At Summer's surprised expression, Granny B gave her another pat. "I've been checking up on your family."

"Oh." She didn't quite know how to take that revelation.

"Feel free to call me an interfering old woman. I promise I won't be at all offended."

"You're an interfering old woman," said Summer.

Which only made Granny B laugh in delight. "Oh, I do like you!"

"Good." She paused. "I think." Then Summer sighed. "I guess you were checking up on me for Harry."

"I was indeed. As I relayed at the farm, he's a good young man, if occasionally a little gormless, but one we're all terribly fond of and would hate to see hurt."

A little bit of steel entered Summer's voice. "I'm not into hurting people." Especially not people who kissed like Harry.

"No, you're not, as I have established. However, you must appreciate that Digby's past misfortune has made me rather protective of my grandchildren and the people they care about. I'm only looking out for them."

Folding her arms, Summer cocked her head to one side. "And what would you have done if you'd found something unsavoury in my background?"

"Very much what I'm doing now." Granny B's clever eyes glittered as she leaned closer. "And then threatened you."

"With what?"

Granny B's eyebrows lifted toward the spa.

"You wouldn't have."

"Yes, I would."

Summer regarded the old woman with disbelief. "You're terrible!"

"I am. Marvellous, isn't it?"

For a long moment Summer was too gobsmacked to comment, then she found herself dissolving into giggles.

Granny B regarded her with fondness. "Now we have that out the way, onto the matter at hand. Has Harry asked you out for dinner yet?"

"Not yet."

The old lady tutted and shook her head. "Silly lad. I did warn him not to listen to Jasmine. The girl has no sense, as made evident by the fact she's sleeping with my grandson. Harry was all for phoning you Sunday morning but she advised it would only make him look desperate."

She sighed. "Poor boy. He was so excited when he returned from seeing you off."

The news left Summer feeling ridiculously warm, although that could have been the sunshine. They had been out in it for a while. She glanced back at the spa. Grace was at the shelves by the window, straightening already regimented lines of product, her mouth mean and the corners of her eyes tight.

"I should go."

"Indeed." Granny B smiled wickedly. She really was the naughtiest lady. "We can't have you upsetting the garbage collector's daughter. Now, don't fret about Gavin. Adrienne and I are onto it and as you've already discovered, we do love a good interfere. Rather livens one's days."

As Granny B strode grandly off, greeting shoppers as she passed, Summer began to muse that maybe she did have someone to share the load with after all. And for the first time since she'd moved to Levenham, she experienced a surge of belonging, that the setbacks of the past were behind her, and a warm future lay ahead.

***

When Summer arrived at Gav's after work that evening, she was confounded to find a small hatchback parked in the drive behind Gav's ute. As far as her experience went, Gav didn't have visitors. She was the only one.

Grace had kept her so busy at the spa — no doubt in retaliation for Granny B's visit — that Summer hadn't had a chance to prepare a meal for Gav. Instead, she'd ducked into the local Woolies for a hot roast chook and a packet of ready-prepared salad mix and dressing to serve with it.

By the time she'd tossed Binky his feed and gathered the shopping bags from the back seat, Summer was fairly itching with curiosity.

"Hello, dear," said the cheerful-looking, slightly plump woman who appeared to have made herself at home in Gav's kitchen. Something tomato-scented was simmering on the stove. Gav was slouched in his usual spot, with a mug in front of him. His chin was jutted, his forearms on the table, fists curled tightly closed.

"Hi," said Summer, not knowing what to make of the scene and feeling awkward with her hands full of supermarket food.

"I'm Vicki," said the woman. "You must be Summer. I've heard all about you."

"Did you do this?" growled Gav.

"Do what?"

He jabbed a finger toward Vicki. "Her."

Vicki swatted a tea towel at him. "Don't you blame Summer. This is something you've brought completely on yourself." She beamed at Summer. "Audrey Wallace sent me."

Summer had no idea who she was talking about and it showed.

"You probably know her as Granny B."

"Oh," said Summer. That answered at least one question, although she was still none the wiser as to the woman's role.

"Here," she said, gathering the bags from Summer and bustling to the fridge where she stowed the goods away. She returned to the table, folding Summer's reusable shopping bags into squares and setting them on the edge in a neat pile. "I'm going to be helping Gavin for a while."

Summer scanned the room. She'd scrubbed it as best she could but Vicki must have put in her own effort. Everything from the taps to the oven gleamed, and the homely aroma of pine and polish drifted in the air. "As a cleaner?"

"Oh no! Although I must admit, I do like things spick. No, dear. I'm here to help Gavin on his path."

Summer blinked. "Path?"

"The twelve steps. AA."

"Oh. Right. Alcoholics Anonymous." Although in this case not very anonymous.

"Best person for it. I'm a recovering alcoholic myself, so I know all the tricks and excuses." She scuttled over to the stove and tucked the tea towel over the rack, then gave one of the pots a stir. "First meeting tonight."

Summer looked at Gav who stared mutinously back.

She went to his side, pulled out a chair and sat down. "It'll help."

"Don't need help."

"You know you do, Gav." She cupped her hand over his arm. "Please, let Vicki help."

To her horror he began to cry. Which only set Summer's eyes bubbling.

"Oh, Gav, don't."

"Let him go, dear. Sometimes you have to hit bottom to climb up."

It broke Summer's heart, watching him sob like that, as if the only thing he had left inside was despair. But perhaps Vicki was right, and it had to happen.

The older lady sat down on Gav's other side. Summer studied her. She didn't look like a drunk. With her greying hair, soft wrinkles and caring eyes, she looked like someone's kindly grandmother. The sort of person who'd bake cakes and biscuits and give lots of cuddles. Not a mean alcoholic, desperate with withdrawal.

Vicki smiled and nodded as if she'd read Summer's mind. "It's true. I was no different. We're very alike, Gavin and I." Her gaze turned downward to where she held her hands clasped, one thumb rubbing the other. "I lost my husband young. He was my best friend. His death completely ripped the life out of me. I'd always enjoyed a glass of wine or two. Mark and I were fond of good food, entertaining with friends, that sort of thing. He kept quite a cellar too. In the weeks after he was gone, when the exhaustion of constant crying had worn off, I found I couldn't sleep." She frowned at the resurrected memories, her voice lowering. "The bed seemed so cold without him, the room so quiet. I started having a drink or two in the evening, just to help me along." Her mouth turned sad, dragging the flesh of her face with it. "It didn't take long for one or two drinks to become a bottle. Then two."

Summer's eyes widened. Two bottles? For a small woman? God. Summer was usually on her ear after two glasses. She checked on Gav, expecting him to be as shocked, but he wasn't. Recognition and resignation dulled his expression, as if the spiral Vicki had followed was as familiar as his own. Most probably it was.

"I started having a drink in the mornings, just to get rid of the shakes. Once you start doing that . . ." Vicki lifted an open palm, her downfall needing no further explanation. It didn't. Gav was living it, while Summer had seen her grandfather and knew where that "remedy" led. "Fortunately, I found AA. It's not a miracle cure, mind. There is no cure. I'll be in recovery for the rest of my life. But without AA I'd probably be dead." She turned to Gav. "Chances are you won't get sober straight away. It took me a year, and that's far from unusual, as you'll learn when you listen to others' stories. It's also hard. Really hard. But the end is worth it. You have no idea how worth it. But you'll never get there if you don't take this first step."

Gav lifted his head and focused on the dresser where his precious photo sat. He didn't say anything, simply stared with liquid, red-rimmed eyes and an expression of such terrible pain that Summer found herself breaking in tears again.

"Time for a bit of dinner, I think," said Vicki. "Then we'll have to head out."

Gav's gaze drifted back to the table and Summer was appalled to notice his fists were once more clenched. Hadn't he been listening? Vicki was offering him a chance, a life. The very things her grandfather never had.

"Please go," she whispered. "For Barbara, and the love you shared."

Finally, he nodded.

***

Summer had been expecting a phone call. What she got was Harry in person, at the spa, bearing half a dozen dark pink roses that matched his flushed face perfectly.

He'd been directed to one of the reception lounge chairs to wait, rising the moment Summer came into view, and scraping a palm down the side of his jeans. He stared at her like a besotted teenager. Her colleague, Megan, who'd been manning reception, had her head studiously bowed over the appointment book but Summer could see she was trying not to laugh.

The newly waxed client she'd been escorting out caught sight of Harry and gaped, before grinning at Summer. "Now that's what I call a big admirer."

Embarrassment left her wanting to crawl under the counter but Summer couldn't help her pounding delight at the sight of him. Harry looked so hopeful and happy, and thrilled to see her. It was hugely flattering and nice, if a little funny. But she was beginning to expect that from Harry. He was like a big affectionate dog that you just couldn't help but adore.

She processed the client as fast as possible and escorted her to the door.

"Have fun," the client said, laughing and waving at Harry, who turned even pinker.

Summer glanced toward the corridor, praying that Grace wouldn't appear. She needed to get back and prepare her room for the next client, but no girl in their right mind would dismiss a man bearing roses. Not one like Harry, anyway.

"Hi," she said, joining him in the small waiting area.

"Hi."

"I thought you were going to call."

"I was, but . . ." He held out the roses. "These are for you."

Summer took them, and pressed her nose to a bloom. They were gorgeously scented. "They're lovely, thank you. And they smell amazing."

"They're from Mum's garden."

"Oh. I hope you asked."

"She picked them for me."

"She must be a good gardener."

"She is."

The conversation went no further. Harry kept staring. A twitchy sort of smile tried to form on his face and fell away, as though losing the courage. Summer tried not to look at the clock but she really couldn't afford to be doing this.

"So . . ." She smiled encouragingly. "You want to ask me something?"

"Oh, yeah. Sorry. Got lost for a minute. Are you, ah, free tonight?"

"I am."

"Would you like to have dinner with me? Josh recommended the restaurant at Ryan's Winery."

"That sounds perfect, but why don't we try somewhere a bit less formal? Say, the Arms?" she said, referring to the Australian Arms, a pub on the main street she'd eaten at a few times. "The bistro's not bad. And to tell you the truth, I could really go a pub steak."

"Oh. Okay. Sure." He didn't sound happy.

"What's wrong?"

"I was kind of hoping to impress you with something better."

"Harry, I share a house with a couple of rabid vegetarians who put on a turn at even the word meat. The last three nights I've eaten tofu stir-fry, quinoa burgers, and a lentil curry that nearly blew my head off. Trust me, a fat rib-eye from the Arms is the stuff dreams are made of."

"Oh. Good. I'll pick you up?"

Summer considered. Having him know where she worked was one thing, giving him knowledge of where she lived was another. Admittedly in a place like Levenham it wouldn't be difficult to find out, but it paid to be cautious. At least in these early stages.

"How about I meet you there?"

She could just about hear the cogs turning in Harry's overactive brain as he assessed her answer. She could tell he wanted to object, but arguing would only make him appear pushy, and Harry was too conscious of his past missteps to make that mistake.

"Okay," he agreed finally. "About six?"

She smiled. "Why don't we try seven? That'll give me plenty of time to finish work, take care of Binky and check on Gav, and make myself presentable."

He brightened at that. "I can help. With Binky, I mean. Not with making you presentable. You don't need any help with that anyway. You could walk through a haystack backwards and still look good to me. Not that you don't look great with makeup and everything."

"Harry."

He grinned sheepishly. "Sorry."

"Don't be. It's nice."

"That's what I'm trying for."

Summer glanced at the clock. "I should get back to work."

It was a major hint but Harry made no move to leave. He was staring again, hesitant and cute. Well, as cute as a man of his size could be.

"Harry?"

Another big sweet grin broke. "I'm going." Then he bent, stopped, cast her a worried look, then bent again to place a gentle kiss on her cheek. He drew back a little, his velvet brown eyes on hers. "See you tonight, pretty girl."

***

Thanks to a client who'd not only arrived late but decided on a different, extended facial to the one they'd booked, it was quarter to six by the time Summer arrived at Gav's. She'd hoped for plenty of time to prepare for Harry. A good bath and loofah followed by a thick slathering of moisturiser to leave her skin soft and scented. Some subtle makeup. Hair that was styled but casual and not too try-hard. Her favourite pale blue capri pants and silky white shirt that revealed just a hint of lacy bra, and a pair of cork platforms to give her height and make kissing Harry easier.

Except that plan was now out the window. The rate things were deteriorating, she'd be lucky to cram in a shower.

After speeding to Gav's, Summer had unlocked the gate as usual and driven through, bemused but not alarmed that Binky wasn't there waiting for her. She'd parked in her usual spot near the tarp, expecting him to come trotting over the hill and arrive at her side by the time she had the door open. When there was still no sign of him after she'd alighted from the car, Summer called his name and listened for a return whinny or at least hoof beats, but there was only the swish of the breeze in the old pines, and warbling magpies.

Only then did a mild form of panic set in. This was wrong. So very, very wrong.

Summer jogged to the top of the hill and surveyed the

other side of the paddock. A few Herefords grazed the paddock beyond, but of Binky there was no sign.

She whirled around to face the other side, checking the ragged fence line, the paddocks across the road. "Please, please."

But the landscape was devoid of anything equine shaped.

With a whimper, she sprinted for Gav's. Her shirt caught on a wire as she climbed through the fence. She ripped herself free. Cool air hit her shoulder as the fabric split open but Summer didn't care. Her horse was missing. The rest of the world could go jump.

"Gav!"

He must have recognised the fright in her voice. The screen door flew open before she could reach it.

"What is it?"

"Binky. Have you seem him?"

Gav peered past her. "He was there earlier."

"He's not now." She bolted again, this time past the side of the house toward the road. At the edge of the drive, she halted, panting, scanning left and right. Then she took off left, stumbling over phalaris clumps, past the paddock gate to trace the ragged road fence. As she reached the end, more whimpers fell from her mouth. Another section had become loose, the wires sagging where they'd fallen from their cleats. The result was a barrier less than knee-high. Not much of an obstacle to a greedy horse.

Summer's breath was coming fast and jagged, each inhalation cutting her throat and lungs. There was plenty of feed nearby. No need for Binky to wander too far. Except she couldn't spot him anywhere.

Gav neared, his face hangdog as he saw the fence. "I should have fixed it."

Fear made her snappy. "Yes, you should have." She rubbed her forehead. Blame wouldn't find Binky. She stared at the road. He couldn't have drifted toward town or she would have seen him. Which meant, unless he'd been horse-napped, he had to have wandered northward.

"Can you call your neighbours for me? Ask if they've seen him?"

Gav nodded. "I'll get onto it."

"Thanks. I'm going to keep looking."

Without a backward glance, Summer broke into a jog.

***

Harry was feeling pretty damn pleased with himself. His shirt was neatly pressed, his jeans clean and his dress boots polished to shiny perfection. He'd even slapped his cheeks with the expensive aftershave his parents had given him for his birthday one year, but had never used.

Eddie had taken one sniff and teased that he stank like a pox doctor's clerk, which would have resulted in a brotherly wrestle had Harry not been desperate to stay tidy. Besides, his mum had promised he smelled nice, and unlike Eddie, he trusted her to tell the truth.

He'd contemplated more flowers but when he'd called over to the homestead that afternoon and suggested it to his mum, she'd smiled fondly, ruffled his hair like he was six, and said that one bunch would do for now. Time to put his Argyle charm into action.

In a romantic mood — a state he leaned toward a lot these days — he'd decided to take Redbank Road into town. Summer would be home by now, getting ready for their date, but it was this road and Binky that had started the whole affair, and seeing Summer's horse made him feel all warm and fuzzy, even if the paddocks the horse grazed didn't.

The clock read six thirty. In his nerves Harry had left home far too early but he wanted to make sure he was waiting at the Arms when Summer turned up. Except this early he'd have a good twenty minutes to fill. Which meant he'd probably have to order a drink and that'd then make him need the loo at some point, which would be embarrassing, nor did Harry want to leave her alone for one second in case some other bastard took the opportunity to try and cut his grass.

What he wanted was to sit close to her, talk, maybe hold her hand a bit when they'd finished dinner. Then, if it went the way he planned, walk her to her car and kiss her again. Not short like before. Long and slow and sexy like.

The idea made him dreamy.

Which was unfortunate because he was barely concentrating when he reached the point where the road cornered back toward Levenham.

Only reflexes had him slamming the brakes and wrenching the wheel in time. That and the gut-horrible terror that if he hit the horse head-on it'd end up through the windscreen and be liable to kill him.

The ute skidded on the gravel. Harry's head banged into the roof as the front driver's side tyre hit a pothole and flung him upward. He felt the tyre burst and the car lose even more traction. Pure strength kept him holding the wheel, but the car was sliding closer and closer to the gutter, though fortunately away from the horse, which had enough sense to skitter in the opposite direction. But that was the only positive. The car hit the steep gutter side-on and tipped, juddering along before sliding to a stop. Harry found himself slammed against the door, dirt and grass slimed across the side window, and regarding the landscape from an angle he'd never previously experienced.

He began to swear. Very, very bad words. Ones he hadn't used aloud since the time he accidentally flipped the quad bike in the creek and broke his wrist in the process. Not that the break was the reason for his curses. It was doing something dumb in front of his dad and Eddie that had caused the verbal assault. And also earned him a smack from his mum after his tattling shit of a brother dobbed.

Tirade over, he blinked and groaned. This was not good. Not good at all.

Casting around, Harry assessed his position and contemplated escape. Passenger side, he supposed. After a quick mental going over to check he was unhurt, Harry unclipped the seatbelt and attempted to crawl across the seats. Only to be stopped by the sudden appearance of a pale face at the windscreen.

Summer.

She was crouched near the fender, one hand on the bull bar, the other trembling over her lips. Her eyes were frantic with distress.

Harry ducked his head and hunched so he could see her properly. A mistake because it only made her burst into tears.

"Summer!"

It was ungainly, and a bit of a struggle, but somehow Harry managed to scramble up and out of the passenger door. The car tilted dangerously under his weight but inertia kept it in place. He tumbled to the road, muttering a "fuck" before rising and dusting himself off.

By the time he was upright, Summer was hovering at the Cruiser's front end, tears streaming over her cheeks and her breath coming in frightened, hiccupy bursts.

"Hey, shh." He enfolded her to him, pressing his cheek to her silky hair and rubbing his big hands over her shaking body. "It's all right. I'm fine." Which, for some reason, only made her cry harder and set an awful thought in Harry's mind. Carefully turning, scared shitless at what he might see, he cast over his shoulder to where he'd last seen the horse.

Harry breathed out. "Binky's fine too. No need to cry. We're all okay."

And he was. Really. Because Summer was in his arms.

***

"Interesting date," Harry remarked, handing Summer another chip.

"Sorry."

"Will you stop saying that?"

"It's a bit hard not to. Binky totalled your car."

"It'll be all right. Bit of panel work. Wheel alignment. It'll be back in action in no time."

Once Summer had calmed and Binky returned to his paddock, Harry had called his dad, who'd arrived twenty minutes later in the farm's workhorse ute with Eddie grinning triumphantly from the passenger seat. Using the winch and a bit of manpower, they had the car out of the ditch in no time. After checking the mechanics were still sound, Harry replaced the tyre and the car was ready.

It was his dad who'd asked Summer what she was going to do about Binky. There was no question of leaving him at Gav's, not with the fence the wreck it was. Summer had stared helplessly at her horse and whispered that she didn't know.

Which then set Harry into action. His solution was to simply float the horse to his vacant house paddock where there was plenty of feed, and most of all secure fencing. Summer hesitated but with no alternative, soon agreed. His dad hitched Summer's aging horse float to the farm ute, loaded up Binky and followed Eddie as he nursed Harry's vehicle slowly home. Leaving Harry to drive a still shaken Summer and her SUV to his place one-handed while he used the other to keep a comforting grip of hers.

Now they were sitting on Harry's verandah, bogging into home-made chips and frozen fish fingers hot from Harry's oven, and watching Binky stuff himself stupid on clover.

Horse and Harry were as smug as one another.

"By interesting, I meant good," he said.

Summer giggled. She had a gorgeous giggle. He could listen to it forever.

"You can't be serious."

"I am."

"You're weird."

Harry stopped chewing. Weird couldn't possibly be promising. Except now he didn't know what to say to make himself appear un-weird, and he thought he'd been travelling pretty well there for a while. Summer had been sweet, admiring his house, helping in the kitchen, teasing him good-naturedly about his culinary prowess. Asking him questions about the farm and his family. Questions he'd answered with not a stutter or ramble in sight.

It was easy at home, with everything familiar and things to be proud of. Summer had seemed impressed too. But now she thought he was weird.

He swallowed, but his mind refused to provide a saving response.

"You're doing it again," said Summer.

"What?"

"Over-analysing. When I said 'weird' I meant in the nicest possible way."

He studied her face. Her blue eyes sparked with a golden tinge from the light, or from amusement. He checked her mouth. Definitely amusement. "I didn't know there was a nice way to be weird."

"There is. And you own it."

That was good. Maybe.

Summer smiled and folded her hands across her belly as she contemplated the sunset, glorious against the undisturbed landscape. She was still in her old jeans but had accepted Harry's offer of a clean polo shirt. The long rip meant hers was only good for rags. Seeing her in his shirt turned him on. A lot. But everything about her did.

"You love it here, don't you?"

He nodded. "Yeah, I do." This place was home. Always would be.

Summer turned away, her gaze wistful. "I miss home. Not as much as I when I first arrived, but the longing's still there."

"Why did you move away?"

"The beauty salon I worked at went broke." The corner of her mouth turned up in a wry smile. "I should have seen it coming, prepared myself a bit, but I was friends with the owner and trusted her. When she went bust I lost a week's wages plus all my holiday pay. She hadn't been paying my super either."

"So, not running from a bikie gang or a murderous ex-husband?"

"No, Harry, nothing like that. Just a girl who loves her chosen career and doesn't want to spend the rest of her life sponging off her parents. So you can stop fretting. I don't have any skeletons rattling around my closet." She threw him a cheeky look. "What about you? Any bunny-boiling exes I should be made aware of?" She wiggled her eyebrows. "A secret sordid past you want to reveal?"

"Sordid?" Harry couldn't help his indignance. He was a good bloke. A bit of a dill sometimes, but not mean or dirty or anything else unsavoury. It kind of hurt she'd think that, even as a tease. "If you're asking whether I'm the sort of man who'd cheat on his girlfriend or ever do anything to hurt her, I'm not. I know I'm not smart like Josh or Digby, but I'm decent and loyal and I take care of my girlfriends. Not that I've had hundreds or anything. I'm not, you know . . ." He blushed, aware he'd probably just made a total twit of himself.

"I know."

Suddenly Summer reached her hand across the table toward him. Heart leaping, Harry took it. He didn't know what it meant only that it signified something important.

Maintaining the connection, Summer rose and moved around the small table to stand in front of him. Harry stood too, his gaze locked on hers. They stood in silence, moths winging around the light, casting shadows.

She smiled. "Harry?"

"Yeah?"

"I think you should kiss me now."

"Okay."

Heart hammering, he did. And this time it lasted. A very long time.

***

Summer grinned at Jas, who was wiping sweat from her face with the bottom of her shirt and complaining again about the heat.

She couldn't blame her. The day was a stinker, but it was the only day they'd all been free for a working bee at Gav's place.

The old bugger had been grumbling all morning too, but Summer knew it was only show. Vicki had whispered how humbled he was by their care and that he felt he'd done nothing to deserve it. Truth was, he hadn't, but that didn't mean they were going to abandon him. And as happy as Binky was at Harry's, Summer couldn't keep exploiting the Argyle's hospitality.

Harry had been appalled when Summer told him she planned to move Binky back to Gav's. Convinced it meant the end of their fledgling relationship, panic had set in. Which for Harry meant half-spoken words followed by gabbling, and then silence when fright shut him up.

Patiently, Summer explained that the move had nothing to do with them. Gav's was closer to town and quicker for her to get to after work, plus the agistment fee gave Gav a little extra money to get things done around the property. He'd been sober six weeks now, and while no one was naive enough to believe he wouldn't lapse, they remained optimistic.

Harry, being Harry, wasn't about to let Binky be moved without first ensuring he was going somewhere safe. Which had given rise to the idea of a working bee.

Emily and Josh, back from their honeymoon spent touring around Ireland and the UK, had immediately volunteered to help, roping in Jas and Digby. Granny B was supervising, cigar clenched in her teeth and feeling superior over her match-making efforts. Harry and Summer were clearly crazy for one another, but she'd also become convinced that Vicki and Gav were developing something beyond AA. The way Summer caught them sometimes glancing at once another, she suspected Granny B might be right.

Lifting the water cooler she was carting around to the workers, Summer moved to the shade near where Harry and Josh were repairing the fence that separated the house and side paddock. She set the cooler down and indulged in a momentary perv, and tried not to sigh mawkishly at her luck.

Despite their less than ideal start, and her initial occasional reservations about his maturity, Harry had proven to be more than grown man enough for Summer. Not only was he kind, generous, affectionate, and pretty damn sensational in bed, he was gorgeous to look at. She didn't even notice his protruding ears any more. They were simply another part of him that she adored.

Harry looked up and caught her watching. He muttered something to Josh and laid down his star dropper, then sauntered over. "You okay?"

"More than okay." She placed her hand on his chest and plucked at the buttons of his faded work shirt. He was warm and sweaty but she didn't mind. "I think you'll deserve a massage after this."

"You do?"

"I do."

They'd had quite a few of those these past weeks. An activity neither had yet to tire of, and Summer suspected they never would.

"You know what'll happen."

"I do." She gave a theatrical sigh. "I sure do, big Harry."

He grinned, then bent down to kiss her. "You say the best things."

"I'm a truthful girl."

"One of the reasons why I love you."

They both stilled with the shock of his admission. Harry's mouth opened then shut, a slightly panicked look fluttering across his face.

Aware he'd need reassurance, and fast, Summer took a breath and grinned. "There are other reasons you love me?"

Relief set Harry's expression dancing. "Countless."

"Name another."

Harry looked over to the gate where Binky was standing, forlornly eyeing the lush paddock across the road. "You have a smart horse."

"A smart horse?"

"Yeah. Really smart."

Summer blinked. Was he serious? He loved her for *her horse?*

"Binky brought us together," said Harry. "That makes him pretty damn smart in my book. Even if he did try to kill me."

"Well then, it's a good thing he didn't, or I'd never have the chance to tell you that I love you too."

"Like I said," whispered Harry as he leaned in to kiss her, eyes blazing in a way that made Summer want to run around yelling her joy at the sky. "Smart horse."

Dear Reader,

Thank you so much for buying and reading *Summer and the Groomsman*. I hope you enjoyed this taste of Levenham and its colourful characters. There are more stories to come!

Would you like to know when my next release comes available plus gain access to exclusive content, news and giveaways ? Please sign up to my newsletter by visiting www.cathrynhein.com/newsletter. If you'd like to find out more about me and my books, including the inspiration behind *Summer and the Groomsman*, you'll find it all at cathrynhein.com, on Facebook and Twitter.

Help others find their next read by leaving a review this novella on your favourite book website.

Now please enjoy this excerpt from *Rocking Horse Hill*, the first of my Levenham Love Stories, and begin your discovery of exactly how Em and Josh found their happiness.

Warm wishes,

Cathryn

Please note: *Rocking Horse Hill* is currently available to Australian and New Zealand buyers only. Other countries coming soon. To keep abreast of when this and other books become available in your region please sign up to my newsletter at www.cathrynhein.com/newsletter.

*Who do you trust when a stranger threatens to
tear your family apart?*

Ever since she was a little girl, Emily Wallace-Jones has loved Rocking Horse Hill. The beautiful family property is steeped in history. Everything important in Em's life has happened there. And even though Em's brother Digby has inherited the property, he has promised Em it will be her home for as long as she wishes.

When Digby falls in love with sweet Felicity Townsend, a girl from the wrong side of the tracks, Em worries about the future. But she is determined not to treat Felicity with the same teenage snobbery that tore apart her relationship with her first love, Josh Sinclair. A man who has now sauntered sexily back into Em's life and given her a chance for redemption.

But as Felicity settles in, the once tightly knitted Wallace-Jones family begins to fray. Suspicions are raised, Josh voices his distrust, and even Em's closest friends question where Felicity's motives lie. Conflicted but determined to make up for the damage caused by her past prejudices, Em sides with her brother and his fiancée until a near tragedy sets in motion a chain of events that will change the family forever.

ROCKING HORSE HILL
CHAPTER ONE

Car headlights shot yellowy-orange streaks over the slick bitumen of Levenham's main street. The footpath remained empty, bar the occasional person dashing for their car, head obscured by a rain jacket hood or low-held umbrella.

Hunched against the wind, Emily Wallace-Jones tucked her leather satchel tighter under her arm and finished locking PaperPassion's shop door. If it weren't for her innate sense of duty she'd have closed up and headed to Camrick and a hearty gossip with Granny B an hour ago, but customers had unexpectedly come in and Em still had rent and other expenses to cover. Nor did she want to develop a reputation as unreliable. Levenham might be home to seventeen thousand people, but word spread just as fast here as it did in a small village, and being a Wallace put her at a big enough disadvantage as it was. In a town where hardship and wealth maintained an uneasy coexistence, old resentments and jealousies lingered.

Rain was sleeting the windscreen of Em's four-wheel drive as she turned into Camrick's drive. The Wallace's 125-year-old manor, where Em's mother, Adrienne, brother Digby and Granny B resided in their distinct quarters, was built on a slight rise several streets back from the centre of town. Night cloaked the property's full grandeur but the lights illuminating the old carriageway exposed part of its handsome front. Compared to some of the rendered brick mansions cropping up around Levenham, Camrick wasn't overly large but, where they had modernity and size, Camrick faced the world with history and majesty.

The house was two storeys. A large bay extended out the left side, decorated columns splitting the three delicately arched windows of each floor. From the bay, the walls sank inwards, protected by a large bull-nosed verandah that wrapped the remaining front and side of the house. The iron-laced second-floor balcony was Granny B's favourite perch. No matter the weather, each evening after dinner she could be found surveying the land and sky through her one good eye, thin cigar in one hand, cut-crystal tumbler of whisky in the other.

The lights in Granny B's rooms were out. Em braked and leaned forward to inspect the stables. The entrance to Digby's lodgings was dark, the wall lights either side of the converted stables' pale blue door unlit. A dull yellow glow peeked from between the blinds of the far right upstairs window – Digby's bedroom. Warmth began to fill her. He was back.

Tuesday-night dinners were a tradition in the Wallace family, an anticipated and fun event. A chance to keep them knitted together, to quickly catch any pull or hint of familial unravelling. When one of them was missing, they all felt it. Even during Em's years at university, no matter what adventure or stress was occurring, Tuesday night would bring a wistfulness for Camrick. Wistfulness soon followed by a crushing yearning for her beloved Rocking Horse Hill.

A gust of wind rocked the car. Granny B's elegant outline was silhouetted against Camrick's rear door. Her grandmother beckoned, the gesture impatient. Em grabbed her bag and the carton of fresh eggs she'd made up before work and made the dash.

Granny B held out a powdery cheek for a kiss. She wore her short hair in its usual style, set crimped and parted on one side, with the waves held in check by half a can of hairspray and a pale metal clip that blended in with her silvery-white hair. She was tall, Em's height, straight-backed and as skinny as a film star. All length and bone with a solid air of haughtiness and privilege. Em had been advised her entire life that she took after her grandmother and had not once minded the comparison. Granny B oozed old-style glamour.

'Ghastly weather, isn't it?' said Granny B. 'How's Muffet coping?'

'A little stiff but the tablets seem to be helping. She's settled in to the house pretty well. If she needs to go outside she comes and wakes me, but that's only happened twice so far. Must have a good bladder.'

'Unlike the rest of us oldies,' said Granny B with a sigh.

Em hooked her arm through her grandmother's. 'You're not old. You're grandly mature.'

Granny B smiled. 'I am rather, aren't I? Incontinence pad and all.' She patted Em's hand. 'Now, come. Digby's got his knickers in a twist about something and your mother and I are anxious to discover the cause. Refused to answer any questions and then scuttled off to the front lounge when we wouldn't be put off. What does the boy expect? Away all that time without once coming home. Barely even rang.'

'Maybe he met a girl.'

'Or boy?' asked Granny B, lasering in on Em with one of her special looks. Chronic open-angle glaucoma had destroyed all but the central vision in Granny B's right eye, causing her to peer at people with unnerving sharpness.

'Would it matter?'

'Not to me.' Her eyes sparkled. 'In fact, it'd be rather serendipitous to see the family wealth pass down the matriarchal line again. Wallace men have had it too easy for too long.'

Granny B steered Em down the softly lit hall, their footsteps echoing off the polished floorboards. A worn Persian runner had once carpeted the hall, which ran the width of the house before hitting a T, one turn leading left to the front wing, the other to the upper floor, but Adrienne had declared the runner a relic of the past and pulled it up. There were plans for carpet and a repaint. Em had always loved Camrick's old-fashioned classicism but her style-conscious mother hankered for modernity, and since Uncle James's death had been slowly transforming the decor.

'Here she is,' announced Granny B as they turned into the kitchen.

Adrienne was at the stove, stirring a pot of something that wafted savoury deliciousness. A light sheen of moisture disturbed her make-up and caused the fine tendrils of her piled-up dark hair to hang limp around her face.

Like all Wallace women, bar herself, Em's mother had an 'A' name. Granny B's was Audrey but a clash with Em's other grandmother, who shared the name, led the children to refer to their grandmothers as Granny A and Granny B. The titles had stuck. Em would have been Amelia except for a last-minute quarrel between her parents – one of many until their divorce – saw the name tradition forfeited, and baby Amelia was instead christened Emily, much to most of the Wallace family's displeasure.

'Sorry I'm late. I got caught up in the *Ballad*,' said Em, referring to her latest calligraphy project, an illuminated edition of G. K. Chesterton's epic poem, *The Ballad of the White Horse*. Em's handmade books helped while away quiet hours in the shop and winter-deadened nights at Rocking Horse Hill and, though it had never been her intention, her hobby was beginning to make money. The last book she'd put up for auction on the Internet – a beautifully scripted and illustrated leather-bound edition of Jules Verne's *Around the World in Eighty Days* – had fetched close to a thousand dollars. People were asking for more, pressing for commission work. So far she'd refused, afraid the pressure would spoil the creative pleasure. Books would come, but at a pace of her own choosing, and driven by inspiration instead of behest. While the extra money helped, Em had proven for several years now that life was survivable on the shop's small profits and income from the share portfolio she'd inherited from Uncle James. Digby allowing her to live at Rocking Horse Hill rent-free assisted a great deal too.

She set down the eggs, smiling as she walked over to her mother. The height gene had skipped Adrienne and

Uncle James' generation, though the Wallace's famous fine bone structure remained. Em inspected the pot of mushroom sauce simmering at the back of the stove, breathing it in. 'Porcini?'

'A few. It's a mix, mainly. Dansley's had some Swiss browns so I threw a handful of those in with the flat tops.'

'Smells amazing.' A ridged cast-iron grill plate was heating on the front hobs, ready for the fillet steaks that were warming to room temperature on a plate nearby. Em counted them. Her mother's boyfriend, Samuel, must be coming. 'Anything I can help with?'

'It's all done. Go through and say hello to your brother while I cook these steaks. See if you can't worm whatever secret he's hiding out of him. Your grandmother's fit to burst.'

'And you're not?'

Adrienne smiled as she left.

Her brother was sitting sideways on the wide sill of the bay window with one leg drawn up and hugged to his chest, staring vacantly outwards as rain pelted the glass and slid in glittery streaks down the pane. The open fire was crackling enticingly, filling the room with warmth and the smell of wood. At the door's opening, Adrienne's drowsy Siamese cat Peaches slid from Uncle James' wingback leather chair – a piece so handsome and well made even Adrienne couldn't bring herself to dump it – to resettle near the hearth.

Em leaned against the doorjamb with her arms crossed, wondering if Digby had even registered her presence. 'Very Heathcliff.'

Digby turned his head. 'Is that good or bad?'

Unlike Em, who had always adored reading and gone on to gain an Honours degree in English from Flinders University, Digby was a left-brained science nerd, who would rather read a paper on plant pollination than *Wuthering Heights*.

'Depends how crazy you turn.' Em crossed the room to join him on the sill. She pushed his leg aside and settled down, pressing her shoulder affectionately against his. 'So, dear brother of mine, I'm guessing good times were had in Adelaide?'

A flush crept up Digby's neck and bloomed pinkly across his cheeks. He crossed and uncrossed his legs at the ankle, tilting forward as if unsure whether to stand or stay sitting. 'They were.'

Em studied him closer. He'd been away on an intensive course at Adelaide University's Roseworthy campus, north of the city, for three weeks. Not an unusual occurrence. As a horticulturalist with the Department of Agriculture, professional development was an important part of his job, but this was the first time he'd not come home for weekends. Adelaide was only four hours or so away, Roseworthy perhaps an hour further. A reasonable drive, but that had never stopped him previously.

He glanced at his watch, twisted the band and frowned at the rain-striped window. Two words for three weeks away. This was going to take some effort.

'Care to fill me in?'

Digby's gaze flicked across the room. Em followed suit and smiled as she spotted Samuel, paused and slightly stooping beneath the doorframe.

'Not interrupting, am I?'

'No,' said Digby, 'not at all.' He leaned closer to Em, his voice low and tainted with smugness. 'All will be revealed after dinner.'

'It had better be or you'll have Gran to contend with.'

Samuel poured himself a drink from the trolley beside the back wall and together they stood near the fire, bemoaning the weather and discussing Samuel's service club's initiatives. He was an attractive man, with salt-and-pepper hair and a rangy body kept fit by morning jogs and golf. He was also a consummate facilitator. The sort of man who went out of his way to relax people – confident and charismatic, but without Em's father's overconfident swagger – and his love for Adrienne was unwavering.

Sadly, the adoration in his blue-grey eyes for Em's mother was tempered by unhealable sorrow. Years before he'd lost his only son to meningitis. For any man the sense of helplessness would be acute, but for a retired radiographer, a man who'd lived his life surrounded by medical science and its wonders, the loss must have held a sharper edge. Which was why, Em supposed, he gave so much of his time to children's services.

Granny B called them to dinner, lingering beside Em to ask if she'd discovered Digby's news. Her mouth puckered upon learning they'd all have to wait.

In an unusual display of fortitude, Digby ignored his grandmother's unsubtle prods and kept his counsel throughout the meal. Samuel filled in the conversational gaps with details of his upcoming trip to Timor-Leste, before discussion moved on to Adrienne's favourite topic of local arts funding, ensuring a lively debate with Granny B and Em over what field should take priority. Em allowed herself a glass of red wine, noting, as did her mother and grandmother, that Digby drank nothing and that his attention was constantly flicking to the dining room's cherry wood mantel clock.

'Well,' said Granny B, dabbing at her mouth with her napkin and looking at Digby, 'we have now finished dinner. What's this news of yours?'

Digby glanced at the clock again. Nearly eight. Em would have to leave for Rocking Horse Hill soon. Even with her heavily blanketed porch basket her darling collie, Muffy, would be feeling the cold. Plus Em needed to lock up the chooks and Chelsea, throw a few sheaves of hay to her horse Lodestone, and check on Kicki and Cutie. The tough little donkeys usually looked after themselves but they didn't have cold-beating rugs like Lod. With the weather this inclement she might need to bring them in.

'Digby?' asked Adrienne, sliding her hand across the table towards his. 'What's the matter?'

The clock began its Big Ben toll. Granny B glared at it as it struck the hours down.

Another sound joined the chime.

Frowning, Em looked at her mother. 'Is that the door bell?'

'I'll answer it,' said Samuel, laying down his napkin and half-rising.

'No!'

Samuel stilled. Everyone's gaze fixed on Digby who quickly scraped his chair back and jerked upright, his napkin falling from his knees to the floor, unnoticed. He stared towards the dining room door with an overexcited, almost fearful look in his eyes.

The clock ceased its chime.

He swallowed, cast around the room and gestured

towards the exit. 'I'll get it.'

For a few seconds, Em, Adrienne, Granny B and Samuel could only gape at the empty doorway before regarding one another with acute puzzlement. Samuel was the first to speak. 'Well, whoever our visitor is, I'm guessing they're for Digby.'

'Shh,' ordered Granny B, her head cocked to listen.

Voices drifted. One deep, the other soft and barely audible. Then Digby and his guest ceased talking, leaving the sound of the ticking clock, the distant drum of rain on the roof, and footsteps on the timber floor, slowly coming closer.

His cheeks blooming with colour, Digby stepped into the room and halted, alone, then inhaled deeply and straightened his shoulders. 'I'd like you all to meet someone.' He took another breath and turned slightly, his arm held out. 'Someone very special.'

A few heartbeats passed, then a small slim blonde woman with her long hair pulled back into a girlish ponytail stepped into his embrace, and together they took another few steps into the room. She smiled hesitantly at Adrienne, then around the table at Granny B, Em and Samuel. Finally her gaze turned back to Digby.

He smiled at her for a moment, holding her like a fabulously rare, priceless and prized piece of art: covetous, careful and proud.

'Mum, Gran, Em, Samuel, I'd like you to meet Felicity Townsend.' He raised his chin. 'My fiancée.'

To discover more about *Rocking Horse Hill* and my other books, please visit cathrynhein.com or your favourite bookseller.

www.ingramcontent.com/pod-product-compliance
Lightning Source LLC
Chambersburg PA
CBHW070312120726
47910CB00007B/2450